Praise for *The Invisible Life of Euridice Gusmao*

'This zesty Brazilian debut has the same brightly coloured quality as a folk painting... A novel that brims indeed with invisible life – not just Euridice's, but the dreams of an entire cast of women: housewives, daughters, and the forsaken who fall in between.'
Daily Mail

'Beguiling... Batalha's empathy is buoyed by puckish wordplay and nostalgia for a time when an act of emancipation entailed a manual typewriter and a good smoke.'
New York Times Book Review

'With something of *Chocolat*'s charm about it, this is a funny, empowering tale of two sisters in forties Rio de Janeiro... A real gem of a book.'
Stylist

'Spellbinding... Batalha is one of those rare writers who can summarise an entire life in a single paragraph, so when she spends an entire book on a single life, the reader is in for a treat.'
Laia Jufresa, author of *Umami*

'With sharp humour and pointed prose, Marta Batalha's novel rebels against the patriarchal forces of her home country.'
World Literature Today

'Tremendous fun... A story of kindness and grace, which does not need to be any longer, but is sufficiently addictive to make us wish it were.'
The Lady

'Batalha's debut shines a light on often-overlooked members of society and paints a thorough and riveting portrait of its characters that will keep readers engaged till the end.'
Booklist

'[Martha Batalha] tells the story of the brilliant sisters Guida and Euridice

he Fire

'Humorous and sensitive... Martha Batalha's mature writing, which is also smooth and intoxicating, seasoned with characteristic authority and jolliness, and an immersive plot, makes this book a narrative delight.' *Asymptote*

'A charming family tale of the Gusmao sisters... For those who enjoy delving into characters and love to watch life unfold for others, this thought-provoking tale will satisfy. A worthy debut for Batalha, full of wry humour.' *Kirkus*

'[Euridice] is scrappy and industrious, and it was a pleasure to get to root for her throughout this novel.' *Book Riot*

'Vibrant and very human.' *BookTrib*

'*The Invisible Life of Euridice Gusmao* is earthy and witty, and the lives of its heroines of everyday existence are memorable and inspiring.' *Foreword Reviews*

'[Batalha] effortlessly brings to life not only her many characters, but the sights, smells and experiences of the world they live in with a deft, wry touch. Characters are at the heart of this enchanting, unusual debut novel which draws readers in with its witty, evocative prose.' *The Herald*

About the Author

Martha Batalha studied journalism and literature in Brazil, working first as a reporter before moving into the publishing industry. *The Invisible Life of Euridice Gusmao* is her first novel. Martha lives in Santa Monica, California, with her husband and two children.

About the Translator

Eric M. B. Becker is editor of *Words without Borders* and a translator of literature from Portuguese into English. He lives in New York.

THE INVISIBLE LIFE OF EURIDICE GUSMAO

Martha Batalha

Translated by
ERIC M. B. BECKER

ONEWORLD

A Oneworld Book

First published in North America, Great Britain and Australia
by Oneworld Publications, 2017
This paperback edition published 2018

Originally published in Portuguese as *A Vida Invisível de Eurídice Gusmão*
by Companhia das Letras, 2016

ISBN 978-1-78607-337-2
ISBN 978-1-78607-173-6 (eBook)

Work published with the support of the Brazilian Ministry
of Culture / National Library Foundation

Obra publicada com o apoio do Ministério da Cultura
do Brasil / Fundação Biblioteca Nacional

MINISTÉRIO DA CULTURA
Fundação BIBLIOTECA NACIONAL

Set in Dante by Tetragon, London
Printed and bound in Great Britain by Clays Ltd, St Ives plc

Oneworld Publications
10 Bloomsbury Street
London WC1B 3SR
England

Stay up to date with the latest books,
special offers, and exclusive content from
Oneworld with our newsletter

Sign up on our website
oneworld-publications.com

MIX
Paper from
responsible sources
FSC® C018072

For Juan, who believed in me from the first
of the four books sacrificed in the name of Euridice.

For my parents, whose presence in everything
I do goes far beyond our family name.

And for the best Portuguese teacher anyone could ask for:
Solveig, this is the same 12-year-old girl
paying back all that you taught her.

Dear Readers,

Many of the stories found in this book indeed took place. Bodies were once piled up in the streets of Rio as a result of the Spanish flu. The verses uttered by Maria Rita have been borrowed from the poet Olavo Bilac, and the news related to her life appeared in the newspaper *Jornal do Commercio*.

Rio also had a bookseller named Garnier – equal parts French and cheapskate – who left his family in a dire financial situation. A very poor young man became rich brewing beer just like Luiz and his Tupã-brand beer (this Luiz was my great-grandfather). Someone did have the singular fate I've given Luiz here, as the writer Luiz Edmundo recalls in one of his books of remembrances.

Heitor Cordeiro, Bebé Silveira, and Raul Régis organized the finest soirées of the newly proclaimed republic. The composer Heitor Villa-Lobos went from school to school teaching the wonders of choral music, and there was indeed a terrific teacher at the Celestino Silva Municipal School, according to my grandfather.

But the parts of this book most faithful to the truth can be found in the lives of the two protagonists, Euridice and Guida. Many like them can still be found. They're the women who show up to Christmas parties and spend the bulk of their time sitting there quietly, with their napkins in their hands. They're the first to arrive and the first to leave. They discuss the seasoning of the cod croquettes, the numerous different desserts and the wine – never drinking too much. They're the ones who ask you how your husband is doing, if their great-niece has a boyfriend yet, or when another great-nephew will be on the way.

The lives of Euridice and Guida have drawn inspiration from the women in my family, and perhaps yours as well.

CHAPTER 1

By the time Euridice Gusmao married Antenor Campelo, the longing she'd felt for her sister's return had already faded. She found herself able once again to flash a smile when she heard something funny, and now managed to make it through two pages of a book without looking up to wonder where Guida might be at that moment. It's true that she continued her search, inspecting each female face on the street, and she was even certain once that she'd seen Guida on a tram headed towards Vila Isabel. Later, this certainty passed, like all others before it.

Why Euridice and Antenor married, no one knows for certain. Some say that the vows were exchanged because José Salviano and Manuel da Costa were already engaged. Others pin the blame for the union on Antenor's sick aunt. By that time, she was no longer able to wash her nephew's clothes with her special lavender detergent. Or make the bits of onion in his chicken soup go unnoticed, which she'd done because Antenor enjoyed the taste of onion but hated its texture. A single camouflaged piece in his beans left him queasy and belching the entire afternoon. There are also those who believe that Euridice and Antenor did indeed fall in love, but that their love lasted for all of one dance at a masked ball at the Naval Club.

The fact is they married, to a packed church, followed by a reception at the bride's house. Two hundred cod croquettes, two crates of beer, and a bottle of champagne for the toast when the time came to cut the cake. The neighbor – a violin teacher – offered to play at the reception. Everyone pushed their chairs off to the side and the couples danced the waltz.

Since Euridice had no friends, there were few young women at the reception: there were two of her aunts who weren't so old, a not-so-attractive neighbor, and another not-so-charming cousin. The most beautiful woman was to be found in the room's only picture frame.

'Who's the woman in this picture?' asked one of the groom's friends.

Antenor nudged his friend: *What kind of manners are those?* The young man looked in embarrassment from side to side, then at the glass in his hand. He set his beer down on the table and walked to the other end of the room.

It was a simple ceremony, followed by a simple reception, followed by a complicated honeymoon. There was no blood on the sheets, and Antenor grew suspicious.

Where on earth have you been? I haven't been anywhere. Like hell you haven't. No, I haven't. Don't go making excuses, you know exactly what we should be seeing here. Yes, I know, my sister explained it to me. A slut, that's what you are. Don't say that, Antenor. I'll say it as many times as I want: slut, slut, slut.

Alone in bed, her body tucked beneath the sheets, Euridice wept softly with each *slut* she heard, with each *slut* the whole block had heard, and because the entire experience had hurt, first between her legs and then inside her heart.

In the weeks that followed things calmed down, and Antenor decided there was no need to take his wife back to her family. She knew how to make the bits of onion disappear, she washed and ironed well, seldom spoke, and had a terrific rear. What's more, the incident on their wedding night served to increase his stature within the relationship, so much so that he looked down on his wife when addressing her. Euridice went along with it. She'd always known she wasn't worth much. No one listing her profession as 'housewife' on the census form could be worth much at all.

Cecilia came into the world nine months and one day after the wedding. She was a smiley and pudgy little baby, welcomed with celebration by the relatives, who exclaimed: 'She's beautiful!' Afonso came into the world the following year. He was a smiley and pudgy little baby, greeted with celebration by the relatives, who repeated: 'It's a boy!'

Responsible for doubling the size of her family in under two years, Euridice decided to retire from her marital duties.

Since she had no easy way to make Antenor accept her decision, she made herself understood by gaining pound upon pound. Extra pounds talk, extra pounds yell, and scream: *Don't you ever touch me.*

Euridice followed breakfast with a ten o'clock snack, lunch with a four o'clock snack, and dinner with a nine o'clock supper. She soon had a triple chin. It looked as if her eyes had shrunk, and her hair could no longer frame her enormous facial features. When she saw she'd reached the right point – the point of making her husband never again come close to her – she adopted more nutritious forms of sustenance. She would diet on Monday mornings, and during the hours between meals.

Euridice's weight soon stabilized, much like the routine of the Gusmao-Campelo family. Antenor would go off to work, the children would go off to school, and Euridice would stay at home, making beef stew and stewing over empty thoughts that made hers an unhappy life. She had no job, she'd already finished her schooling – how was she to fill the hours of the day after tidying up the beds, watering the plants, sweeping the living room, doing the laundry, seasoning the beans, cooking the rice, making the soufflé, and frying up the steaks?

The thing is, Euridice was brilliant. Give her the proper equations and she would design bridges. Give her a laboratory and she would invent vaccines. Give her blank pages and she would write classics. But instead, she was given dirty underwear, which she washed quickly and left spotless, before sitting on the couch, looking at her nails, and thinking about what she ought to be thinking about. That's how Euridice decided she shouldn't think at all, and that in order to not think she ought to keep herself busy every hour of the day. There was only one household activity that brought such a benefit, given it was nearly endless in its daily demands: cooking. Euridice would never be an engineer, would never step foot in a lab, and would never dare to write verse, but she dedicated herself to the only activity with a little something of engineering, science, and poetry.

Every morning, after waking up, getting ready, feeding and getting rid of her husband and kids, Euridice would open the *Aunt Palmira Cookbook*. Duck à l'orange made for the perfect dinner, since she would have to buy duck and there were no oranges at home. She would throw on a dress to go out and head to the poultry market to pick out a healthy-sized duck. She took advantage of the opportunity to buy a chicken, since the duck had to spend the night soaking in wine and spices, which meant that day's dinner would also provide a challenge. The recipe called for a young, plump duck, the chicken needed to have a red comb and a meaty breast. At the market Euridice would grab oranges for the following day, coconut flakes for a cornbread cake, prunes for the stuffing, and a dozen bananas for Afonso and Cecilia, for after they played with their food and cried: *I don't like it.*

Arriving home, she would string up the chicken and the duck by their legs, cut their throats, and then attend to her other chores while the blood ran into the sink. The duck and the chicken were scalded for two minutes, their feathers plucked after the body cooled, a flame passed along the skin to singe the little hairs. The innards and the gizzard, liver and heart were removed with a tiny cut along the belly before roasting the entire bird, or through a large incision in the middle of the body if the dish called for it to be chopped.

There were also the side dishes. She never simply fried the potatoes, but stuffed them with ham and cheese or added spices and breadcrumbs and deep-fried the whole thing. Her rice was never just white, but adorned with raisins, peas, carrots, tomato sauce, coconut milk, or one of a dozen other ingredients suggested in her cookbook. Custard in a plum sauce, cascade meringues, coconut candy – whatever her cookbook told her, the young housewife did, and everything the young housewife did, she did with flare.

Euridice's culinary prowess went unrecognized by her family. Afonso and Cecilia had a phase where they sang an ode to pasta, and Antenor wasn't the kind of man to be impressed by sea bass with clam sauce. *Give us some spaghetti*, the children would say. *Make me a nice steak*, Antenor would chime in, and Euridice would head back into the kitchen to boil water for the spaghetti, promising Antenor a filet mignon free of saffron. After two or three nights of simpler food, she'd return to her cookbook, and surprise her family with pork medallions in rosemary sauce.

When she'd had a go at all the recipes, Euridice thought the time had come to create her own dishes. While Aunt Palmira knew a great many things, she didn't know everything, and

Euridice had a sneaking suspicion that creamed yucca could serve as a topping for jerky, that guava paste would go well with chicken Milanese, that stuffing could be replaced by this curry seasoning she found in the specialty market, but which was not mentioned in her cookbook. One Thursday morning she put on a dress and off she went to the stationery store on the corner.

'Good morning, Dona Euridice.'

'Good morning, Antonio.'

'Looking for something special?'

'A big, ruled notebook.'

Antonio pointed to the pile of hardcover notebooks on the shelf. Euridice entertained herself with the choice and Antonio entertained himself with Euridice. Perhaps because he had spent his childhood sleeping amid the bountiful flesh of Chica de Jesus, the black nursemaid responsible for raising Antonio and his brothers while their mother attended Rio's most exclusive soirées, Antonio found much to like in Euridice's bountifulness. He also liked her eyes, her pointy nose, her tiny hands, the delicate pendant around her neck, her chubby ankles, and just about every other part of her his eyes could see.

Euridice took her time with the notebooks. As it was to be *her* recipe book, she needed to choose the best among the identical ruled notebooks. She leafed through one of the notebooks, found a wrinkled page and placed the notebook back on the pile. She grabbed another, saw a smudge on the cover and put it back on the pile. She looked over a third and found no defects. She was about to deliver the Chosen One to Tinoco, the boy who had been working at the store since forever, when Antonio quickly offered himself to help her check out. They discussed the weather while Euridice waited for her change. She left without realizing that her commentary on the recent rain had been the high point of the man's week.

On her way back, Euridice hummed a tune, happy as could be. She quit humming and lost some of that joy when she heard *Good morning, comadre!*

It was Zélia, the next-door neighbor. Zélia was a woman with many frustrations, chief among them the fact that she wasn't the Holy Spirit, able to see and know everything. She was closer to the Big Bad Wolf, because she had big eyes to see with, big ears to hear with and a big mouth, which spread the neighborhood news up and down the block. Zélia also had a turtle's neck, which seemed to stretch from inside her collar any time she saw someone of interest pass by her house. The woman was stranger than a platypus, and if a person like her didn't call much attention, it was because Zélia was merely one among many of the same stripe living in that time and place.

'Replenishing the stock of school supplies for the children?'

Euridice pulled the package to her chest, in a dubious gesture. She wasn't sure whether she was protecting her chest, or the package.

'Good morning, comadre. This? Oh, it's just a notebook… to keep track of household expenses.'

The next day, all the women on the block bemoaned the fact that Euridice and Antenor were facing financial troubles. *Well, what do you expect?* asked Zélia. Euridice had no limits when it came to her grocery shopping, and how many times could one go to Casas Pedro in search of spices? The scents coming from that kitchen! Exotic aromas, so different from the rice and beans found at the other houses on the block. Sooner or later, she'd have to face reality.

Since she couldn't be the Holy Spirit, Zélia contented herself with a lower post, proclaiming herself prophet. Her empirical observations yielded precise prognostications, which had the common characteristic of being gloomy. *That one there is going to drag her husband into bankruptcy*, she decreed with her pointy chin.

Zélia hadn't become a platypus just like that. It's known that such evolutions take their time. The transformation began while she was still a child, when what should have been a blessing became a curse. From her father she inherited a taste for the news, from her mother, a life restricted to home. The world had brought her heartbreak; fate brought her a lack of options. That's how her gossipy nature came about.

Whoever met the young lady would not believe that her stern eyes had once been capable of gazing without malice, whoever saw her sneering smile would never imagine that it had once been just a smile. But that's exactly what Zélia was like as a child: all smiles and kind looks. During the few years she was happy, she'd thought life was something so incredible that she complained when bedtime rolled around, refusing to sleep. *I can listen to the crickets, I can identify the sounds around the house, I can think about what to do in the morning, and what games to play in the afternoon*, she would say to herself, eyes wide open in the dark. Every night, exhaustion got the best of her. She would fall asleep, but she soon discovered that she'd been duped and was always the first to wake up in the morning.

Zélia woke singing, ate with a smile, and skipped rather than walked. She made up dances, blew kisses, and laughed for laughing's sake. Everything looked fun to her – picking out the little stones from the beans, folding the dry clothes from the line, finding spider webs on the ceiling, and sweeping the corners of the living room.

The neighborhood women disapproved of the girl's impulsive actions – *That's a lack of a good belting, that's what that is.* But her mother paid no mind to such advice. 'One day she'll discover that life isn't how she imagines it, but that day doesn't have to come today,' she said, filled with nostalgia at seeing in her daughter's skipping and jumping her own childhood, many years earlier.

For Zélia, every day was great, and Saturday the greatest day of all. That was when she would see her father for the first time all week. Alvaro Staffa was a newspaper reporter by day and a carouser by night. By the time he arrived home, his children were already sleeping; when he woke up, they'd already gone off to school. His fatherly duties were fulfilled on the weekends, when he had to entertain the kids while his wife prepared lunch. Alvaro would scratch his head, looking uneasily at his kids, and prepare himself to do the only thing he knew aside from writing and drinking, which was to talk about what he'd written and what he still might write. He would set Zélia on one knee and put Armandinho on the other, sit Francisco off on one side, place Zezinho on the other and tell Carlos, Julieta, and Alice to sit cross-legged on the floor, before closing the bedroom door so as not to wake the youngest. He then would tell his children about his adventures as a reporter.

One day he was at the Copacabana Palace together with the Miss Rio contestants, the next he was in Niterói assessing the damage caused by an accident with fireworks. There was the lunch in the Café Paschoal to honor the president, the debate about the extinction of hand-pulled carts in the streets downtown. The golden plaque given to Santos-Dumont by his friends and the much-anticipated bazaar at the Church of Bom Jesus do Monte. The decrees signed at the transportation department, the fire that razed a shack on the Avenida do Mangue, and the arrest of that blind musician, the one who could always be found on Rua Direita and had twins to raise. His arrest was a bunch of nonsense, which only served to show the cruelty of the police.

It was the only time of the week when peace came to the house. Besides Alvaro's voice, the only noise was that of the pressure cooker.

Until one day Zélia's mother's prophecy came to pass. The girl underwent two tragedies that put a stop to her skipping and jumping. The first was her father's death. The second was the discovery that she was ugly.

Alvaro Staffa discovered his calling as a reporter at fifteen. At that time, he was already a graduate and postgraduate of the streets of Rio. At eight years of age, he arrived from Italy with his parents; at nine, he became an orphan. How he learned Portuguese, how he learned to read and write, how he didn't die of starvation, the plague, or a stab wound is a mystery that can only be explained by serendipity. He sold candy on the ferry and lottery tickets at the trolley stop. He shined shoes, washed windows, and delivered papers. He eked out his survival from small jobs on the street and the favors he performed for a respectable type in a suit, who took him to a hotel room in Lapa once a week and asked him to walk nude across his back while singing 'O Sole Mio.'

Before he reached the age of thirteen, he'd been arrested nine times. He knew how to wield a razor blade, and was feared for his capoeira skills. Feeling that it was time to settle down, he traced out a career plan, which consisted of trying for a promotion. From a delivery boy Alvaro became an office boy in the newsroom. An unthinkable leap forward. It was the first time he'd worked with a roof over his head.

The promotion came not a minute too early. For some months now, Alvaro's services as a nude singer had no longer been required, due to his being too heavy to walk on the back of the man in the suit. And such privileges he now enjoyed – he had his very own desk, and when he had no tasks to do he could spend the entire afternoon sitting down in the company of a book.

This good life came to an end in the winter of 1918, when the city recorded its first cases of Spanish flu. At the beginning, it was one here, one there. A week later, it was many here, and even more there.

By October, half of Rio's population had fallen ill. One Wednesday morning, only Alvaro, the newspaper's editor, Camerino Rocha, and the typographer showed up to the newsroom. Camerino looked over at the boy behind the desk, asked if he could write, and sent him to the street with a pencil and a notepad.

Alvaro spent three hours walking the streets of Rio. He saw men in agony as they vomited blood and children talking to mothers who had already died. Sick people in a delirium, expelled from their homes. Long-bearded prophets proclaiming the end of the world. He heard the screams that preceded death coming from behind closed shutters and counted hundreds of bodies in the streets. In vain. As soon as he'd finished counting, someone else would turn up dead, or the wagon sent by the city government showed up to tow away the bodies. With the wagon scarcely gone, fresh bodies could soon be found on the doorsteps, waiting for the hour that came after the hour of death, the time to enter the competition for space in one of the city's communal graves, which were being dug every day.

In the weeks that followed, this would be his routine: arrive in the newsroom, grab a pencil and notepad, go out to document the unfolding tragedy and come back with more than enough stories to fill the day's paper. He seemed immune to the illness and the horrible scenes before him. Why his body resisted is anyone's guess; his spirit resisted the images because he'd watched his entire family perish, victims of yellow fever.

When the reporters who survived the flu came back to the newsroom, they found Alvaro in front of a typewriter. With the exception of weekends and Christmas Day, the cub reporter could be found in the same place every day and for hours on end, a routine he would maintain until the day he died.

How did Alvaro die? There are two versions of that story. The first is that he began to feel a terrible thirst, which caused him to re-evaluate his priorities. Before the onset of this thirst, his time with his kids, haircuts, birthday parties, what he'd had for breakfast, what he would have for dinner, all these were irrelevant details that took place between what was really important: writing, talking about what he'd written, and drinking so he could speak at even greater length about the things he'd written and the things he might yet write. For this new Alvaro Staffa – the one with an unquenchable thirst – the priorities were drinking to put up with his wife and kids, drinking before and after getting his hair cut, attending birthday parties to drink more, and drunken babbling about what he'd written recently.

He could just about make it to the newsroom hung over. He'd catch some grief from Camerino, and to set himself right he began to snort cocaine. The pure stuff, German, direct from the Merck labs, bought on the black market behind the Hotel Glória.

The primary consequence of this change in Alvaro could be seen in the family pantry. Up until then, the pantry was stocked according to a certain logic: it started off full and was empty by the end of the month. After Alvaro began to fall apart, every day seemed like the end of the month. All that remained was a handful of flour, some leftover sugar, a few beans, a single onion. A banana had managed to escape the children's hunger and turned brown, and in their misery, the family debated whether they should eat the half-rotten fruit.

Alvaro died of cirrhosis at thirty-five. Those of Alvaro's friends who subscribed to this version of his death spent the wake lamenting the devastating addictions that cut down the country's greatest talents in their prime.

There is also a second version of this story, in which Alvaro Staffa, this self-made man who raised himself up from nothing – this man who was straight as an arrow, lost his direction, and straightened out again after marrying – continued to harbor certain dubious tendencies. Alvaro liked life on the street, and the people who could be found there. Now and then, the young man would fall for a mixed girl – it had always been the mixed-race girls he found most appetizing. Later he'd fall out of love once more, and life would go on.

Such were his intentions when one Shrove Tuesday he met a samba dancer marching along in a Carnival bloc. She had teeth as white as the white of her eyes, even if it wasn't possible to see her eyes: Rosa danced with closed eyes and wide-open smile, shaking her hips in a way Alvaro had never seen. Those were hips with personality. Firm, taut, strong, and irresistible.

It took Alvaro three months to properly examine those hips, which he did in Rosa's boarding-house room. The couple spent entire afternoons exchanging bodily fluids and vows of love, Rosa begging Alvaro to whisper Italian in her ear, Alvaro begging Rosa to parade around nude. Rosa gave herself entirely to the affair. Alvaro gave his penis entirely to the affair.

Until one day Alvaro took his penis and his Italian cooing and left the boarding house. Back home, his wife had already healed from the latest birth, which meant he'd have other ways to fulfill his needs. He said goodbye to Rosa like he might to a great-aunt: knowing he'd never see her again and without much caring.

Rosa couldn't handle the abandonment. She broke vases, tore up clothes, and considered rat poison. She lost so much weight that in addition to Alvaro she also lost her hips. She soon gained bags under her eyes, disheveled hair, and dismissal from her job as a waitress at one of the taverns on Rua Direita.

It all would have ended there, with Rosa chewing over the bitter loss of her first love, had she not been the daughter of Oluô Teté, one of the most respected Candomblé priests in Rio. His shrine in Vila da Penha attracted important politicians from across the country. Carriages coming from Botafogo would stop in front of his gate, and out stepped aristocratic ladies with their faces concealed by hats and hidden behind fans. Oluô Teté knew how to revive the sick and converse in the language of the dead. He knew how to channel the spirits and to summon sun and rain.

Seeing his daughter in that state, Oluô did what any father would do: he clenched his fists and wished the dago an eternity spent burning in hell. In his case, his wish was easily fulfilled, since he had a direct line to proper sources. Oluô had a cow killed and asked Rosa to bring him the bedsheets she had shared with Alvaro. He swaddled his daughter in the blood-stained sheets and began to pray or sling curses in some unfamiliar dialect. The drums of the Morro do Cariri slum never ceased playing the entire weekend.

On Monday morning, Alvaro began drinking.

Rosa's hate was so strong and her father's magic so potent that the curses cast over Alvaro affected all who were product of his seed, putting at risk the lives of his eight children and sixteen bastard kids all over the north side of Rio.

João died the same month as his father. He curled up in his father's empty bed and cried for three straight days until he was consumed by grief. Julieta fell ill two weeks later. The doctor diagnosed polio and said she'd never walk again.

His widow and remaining children don't like to remember these months of misery. What is known is that Carlos, then thirteen, became the man of the house. And that the sloths of Campo de Santana began to disappear around the same time the family had its first taste of exotic meats.

Soon after, they were taken in by a relative living in the working-class neighborhood of Bangu – the house had five rooms and one bathroom, an image of Jesus Christ guarding the doorway, chickens and mango trees in the yard. Zélia's family was given a room and the last spot in line for the bathroom.

When Zélia went to live with her relatives she still had the blue notebook her father had given her. *This is for you to write what you think about the world*, he'd said to her. Zélia's little arms had clasped Alvaro's neck, who, with eyes closed, gave thanks to God for the family he'd been given. The clumsy sentences of the first pages soon evolved into elaborate paragraphs, written throughout those months of suffering. Writing was Zélia's only solace. A solace that she stashed beneath her mattress, later to be found by her cousins, who, between giggles, read a few passages aloud before dinner. This raised the ire of Zélia's mother, who defended her daughter with attacks on her nephews, and who was attacked in turn by her brother. *Who did she think she was, besides someone who lived off charity?*

Later, when Zélia left her aunt and uncle's house, the notebook was long gone. It went straight into the trash, as Zélia harbored the illusion that if the notebook were buried in the trash, it might take her cousins' mockery with it. It had all been a bunch of nonsense anyway.

Zélia managed to endure a lot. She endured the patched clothes and the second-hand panties. She endured the same shoes she'd worn for so many years, loose around her ankles in the beginning and pinching her toes by the end. She endured her cousins' laughter and the lack of affection from her mother, who was always worn out after doing the laundry and cooking for the fifteen people at their new home. She endured the watery soup, and the cries of her younger siblings.

But she couldn't endure adolescence. When she discovered two bean seeds behind her flat chest, when she had stomach cramps accompanied by bleeding, when she felt unprecedented desires and fears, her unbendable optimism bowed.

Zélia's mouth is big as a house, Zélia's mouth is big as a house, was her cousins' new refrain.

One afternoon when there were only a few people at home, she went into the bathroom. She locked the door and examined her face in the mirror. What she saw was no longer the face of a slightly crossed-eyed child with a huge hair bow hanging across her temple. It was the face of a girl with ill-behaved hair, ill-proportioned eyes and nose, pimples dotting her ill-fitting forehead and a huge mouth full of lips and teeth. It was an abundant, unnecessary, excessive mouth. Two thick lines that cut mercilessly across her face. As Zélia stood there, she arrived at the conclusion she'd hold on to for the rest of her life: she was ugly.

It was written in her fate and on her face that she would be unhappy. The desires and fears she'd gained growing up mixed with a newfound bitterness, which sprouted from her chest like weeds. Even in the early years of adolescence, when Zélia still told herself it was silly to think like that and plucked the bitter little weeds one by one, they grew back unrelentingly and multiplied. Until one day Zélia stopped plucking them, looked once again into the mirror, and decided that the ugliness of her face and the sadness brought by living were perfect companions to the bitterness she felt in her heart.

That's when the new Zélia was born. The only thing she inherited from the old Zélia was enthusiasm for life, now distorted. She would now classify others according to a cruel system devised to make sense of the world. Zélia didn't want to be, and wouldn't be, the only one who was unhappy. From that moment on she was able to find unhappiness everywhere, through things both real and simply rumored, which she spread far and wide with her enormous mouth.

Zélia had one last glimpse of hope, when she imagined a better life. It was shortly before her eighteenth birthday. For some months she had been trading letters with a distant cousin on her father's side, a certain Nicolas Staffa, who had settled down with his family in the southern part of the state of Minas Gerais. Nicolas's father was an entertainment impresario who was quickly becoming an influential person in the city of Lambari. One day Nicolas wrote to Zélia to tell her that he was coming to Rio on account of his father's business, and that he would take advantage of the trip to stay until the holiday ball at the Clube dos Democráticos. Would Zélia and her sisters like to come along? Zélia wrote back a shy but enthusiastic response: of course, they would love to go.

Zélia Staffa, Zélia Staffa, the young girl repeated to herself with a smile. Life was full of irony. In the months before, she'd been pairing her first name with the last name of all the boys she knew: Zélia Camargo, Zélia Cavalieri, Zélia Calixto. Who would think that among so many possible combinations her name would simply remain Zélia Staffa. *Zélia Staffa.* The name suited her.

By that point, Zélia was well aware of the size of her mouth and all the other causes for displeasure that surrounded it. But she had found hope in this exchange of letters with Nicolas, for two reasons: the first is that they'd already met, which meant the young man had freely chosen to continue their correspondence, even after becoming acquainted with the generous proportions of her face. The second is that when Zélia put pen to paper, she transformed into one of the most interesting women of her time.

Zélia thought of nothing but the dance. She sang softly, practiced braiding her hair, and during those few days she flashed the very last smiles that recalled those of her childhood. She sewed her own dress, a light pink outfit with a flared skirt and puffed sleeves. She sewed a bolero jacket from ivory-colored fabric, to be worn when entering and leaving the dance. She bought new gloves, bought a hat to be paid off in installments, and borrowed her oldest sister's earrings. She followed the beauty tips found in the *Young Ladies' Journal*. She rested her eyes behind cucumber masks, she left her hair soaking in aloe vera, and added iodine drops to the bathwater to give her skin an amber tone. On the day of the dance, Zélia was so happy she even felt beautiful.

But the dance didn't go well. The Nicolas at the dance seemed different from the one she knew from their letters. He was polite but restrained. Cheerful but reserved. Their conversations died after the third exchange. There was a great distance between them, even greater than the distance between Lambari and Rio, which they'd managed to bridge so well during their months of correspondence.

At some point in the middle of the evening, Zélia gave up her hopes of hours of enjoyment like those spent reading Nicolas's letters. She left the young man standing in the middle of the ballroom, saying she had to retouch her make-up. Nicolas didn't so much as say 'uh-huh', he only nodded his head. Zélia turned her back and broke into tears. The interesting Zélia, or the interesting Zélia she had thought she was in Nicolas's eyes, gave way to a sad and insecure girl. With each step towards the bathroom her insecurity grew. When, on the way, she checked herself out in the wall-length mirror, all she could see was a crooked skirt, obnoxious puff sleeves, and a mouth as big as a house.

The paucity of Nicolas's words changed the way Zélia thought of herself. She was sure no one at the dance would like to be at her side. She had no idea how to dress. Her curls weren't as curly as they should be. The rouge that had given her a special something had already faded. And that red lipstick – why had she decided to use red lipstick? That lipstick attracted more attention than a traffic light. Zélia looked for a chair in the corner of the room and stayed there the rest of the night. She wished she could disappear, which was impossible. She could never disappear with a mouth like hers.

But Zélia's biggest mistake that night wasn't the dress, the hair, or the lipstick. Sitting in the corner of the room was Plinio, a young man with a skinny neck and a pained expression on his face, as though he constantly had the urge to take a pee. Plinio was accustomed to sitting in corners, and he felt right at home in that one. When Zélia sat down next to him, he didn't see a girl with half-undone curls or an oversized mouth. He saw only a girl who, like him, preferred to sit in the corner.

They married the following year. Plinio Correia would, for forty years, perform the same job as manager in Rio de Janeiro's Electric Light Company. His salary would never be magnificent or deplorable, his ambitions would waver between nonexistent and irrelevant. He expected nothing from life beyond perpetual motion – as far as he was concerned, the unknown always constituted a threat. The most adventurous thing to happen to Plinio was a five-day bus trip to Iguaçu Falls. He and Zélia would grow old in the most common way of growing old; getting more distant every single day.

At first, Zélia saw marriage as the solution to her unhappy days in Bangu. Later she saw marriage as a mistake. A mistake who snored loudly by her side every single night. When she watched Plinio sleeping with his mouth wide open, Zélia would think about the mediocrity of her life. She thought about Nicolas, she thought about how she should have made more of an effort that night at the ball. She thought about how she might have been the Casino Queen of Lambari instead of the wife of some nobody in Tijuca.

What Zélia never learned was that Nicolas hadn't kept a distance that night due to some poor intellectual display or her less-than-perfect looks. What happened was that the young man, accustomed to a dozen or so single young women in Lambari, had an overdose of sensations upon finding so many interesting Rio girls at the Clube dos Democráticos. *This city is paradise*, he'd thought to himself. He encountered little difficulty in re-evaluating his priorities, placing marriage at the bottom of the list and putting a few years of experimentation at the top.

Perhaps it was due to the curse of Oluô Teté (who, after growing disillusioned following eight failed trysts, lost his patience and put a spell on all the women in Rio). The fact is that ever since Rosa's mother's time, the women of Rio have been forced to confront the curse of being so beautiful, so intelligent and so numerous, that the men of the city have the luxury of not needing to choose just one.

That's how Zélia came to live in Tijuca, fully aware that she would never ever leave. It wasn't a bad place to be. It was much better than the tiny room in the back of the house in Bangu. But Zélia wasn't able to see the gifts life brought. She could only see her average husband, her unremarkable kids, her plain old house. The girl who had once carried around a blue notebook continued exploring the world around her in order to uncover shortcomings only she could see.

If a neighbor didn't say good morning, it wasn't because she hadn't seen Zélia, but because she had ignored her. If the guava she bought had worms, it was because the seller wanted to pull one over on her. If Dona Irene gained weight, it was because she was unhappy; if she lost weight, it was because she'd become depressed. If the baker's daughter worked the cash register, it was because she wanted to nab a husband; if she wasn't helping it was because she was thick-headed. If her god-daughter earned good grades it was because she was a show-off; if she hid her report card, she had no brains.

And what about you, don't you know how to do anything except listen to the radio? Zélia crossed her arms and turned her nose up as she addressed her husband, the mistake.

Seated in his corner, Plinio didn't respond. He was plagued by the affliction that assails so many men: the vow of silence after a few years of marriage. By the time of their fifteenth anniversary, his burps outnumbered his syllables uttered.

At some point, Zélia's constant dissatisfaction began to modify her appearance. When cutting the squash, unclogging the sink, dusting the top shelves, Zélia made all sorts of grimaces, which in the beginning were out of place, but later became permanent features.

She soon had dark circles under her eyes, the result of nights of little sleep. If as a child Zélia waged war against sleep, in the years following her marriage she simply could not doze off. Oh, what good just a bit of sleep would do in this tedious little life of hers! No such luck. Zélia spent more and more nights laying awake, which only increased her dark circles and foul mood. The sleepless nights so coveted during her naïve years became a burden to be carried for the rest of her endless days.

After some time, when Zélia looked in the mirror, she could no longer tell if she was embittered because she was ugly or if she was ugly because she was embittered. Her escape was the window. There she could see everything beyond her painful reality. And that's where she saw Euridice, this young lady who didn't seem to be entirely at ease and who was most deserving of the judgment that Zélia knew only too well how to dish out.

They'll be bankrupt before we know it. Mark my words: Euridice knows how to throw banquets, but a few years from now she'll be living off crumbs.

CHAPTER 2

Since her financial woes existed only in the heads of others and not in her household budget, Euridice continued with her plans. She dreamed up cakes, tried out new soups and worked up original sauces, carefully noting the recipes in her notebook. That notebook was her diary. The account of all she did to bear her domestic exile, to transform the walls of that house into something less oppressive.

Some months later, Euridice's right-slanted handwriting had filled the entire notebook, and she thought it was time to show it to her husband. She prepared a special dinner with one of the dishes Antenor liked: turkey medallions in Madeira sauce.

The day before the dinner she went to the poultry market to buy the turkey. She walked back home with the bird in her hand and Zélia looking on from a distance, indignant because it wasn't yet Christmas Day. Euridice set the turkey loose on the patio and went inside to prepare the bowl of cachaça she'd give to the animal before slaughtering it. The alcohol would calm the bird and ensure its meat was tender. She closed the liquor cabinet and leaned against it. Her recipe book was done; she wanted to publish it, and – who knew? – maybe write another one. She'd have her own radio show, perhaps even a column in the *Young Ladies' Journal*! She'd offer cooking and baking courses for newlywed women. Her wide eyes opened even wider. It was within reach; she need only speak with Antenor. Yes, she need only speak with him. Her eyes returned to their normal size. She took two swigs of cachaça before serving the bowl to the turkey.

On the Night of the Great Feast, Antenor returned home at five-thirty in the afternoon, as he always did. He kissed his wife on the forehead before heading for the bedroom to change his clothes. He put on his slippers and went back downstairs for dinner. Aromas even more extraordinary than those that typically escaped from Euridice's kitchen wafted through the dining room, the bedrooms, and the house next door, prompting Zélia's husband to complain: 'Leftover soup, again?'

When he saw the Italian tablecloth and wine glasses reserved only for special occasions, Antenor was caught by surprise. When he saw the four-course meal – with his favorite turkey medallions *with that brown thing on top* – his surprise grew. But he was even more surprised with his wife's lack of appetite. Euridice sat quietly by his side during the meal, and served dessert to the children in the kitchen.

When Antenor was halfway through his citrus pavé she poured herself a glass of wine, took a gulp, and placed the notebook on the table.

'Look at this, Antenor,' she said, pushing the notebook towards her husband. 'All my recipes are in here. Do you think I could publish it?'

Antenor set his plate aside. He burped discreetly and began leafing through the notebook. Euridice sat there motionless, listening to the rustling of pages, until her husband broke out in laughter.

'Stop kidding around, woman. Who buys a book written by a housewife?'

Her husband's laugh entered in one ear and never went out the other. She lowered her head, began fidgeting with the ruffles of her apron and tried to explain. She'd been cooking for years, and the dishes seemed to be quite good. But Antenor had no patience for chitchat. He returned to the matter he considered to be truly important.

'Pass me the toothpicks.'

And Euridice, who had never known life beyond those walls, or beyond her parents' house and neighborhood, figured her husband was right. Antenor knew things. He had studied accounting, he was an employee of the Bank of Brazil, and discussed politics with other men. When she was working on her recipes, she had been certain she was doing something meaningful, but now, before her husband, everything seemed worthless. Publishing a book, having a radio show – all fantasy. The one with vision in the family was Antenor – a vision defined by everything he saw from the trolley on his way to work. But even this limited vision was greater than any that could come from Euridice, who never saw beyond the walls of her house, the local market, the grains in the cupboard, and the overwhelming emptiness that gnawed away inside her.

The rest of that evening was like any other. Mother and daughter cleaned the plates from the table while Antenor and Afonso went to the living room to listen to Radio Nacional. Euridice washed the dishes without looking up. A tear or two mixed in with the dishwater.

'Is this good, Mommy?'

Standing on her tiptoes on top of a stool, Cecilia helped her mother dry the dishes.

'Yes, Cecilia. One day you'll make a terrific housewife.'

The last thing Euridice took from the table was her notebook. She ran her fingers over the cover, then raised her head and turned her eyes away. She tossed the notebook into the trash, where it landed atop bits of pavé.

Two hours later, Antenor was breathing loudly and Euridice tossed and turned among the bedsheets. That man, she knew, was a good husband.

Antenor never disappeared for days and never lifted a hand to her. He brought in a good salary, complained very little, and conversed with the children. The only thing he didn't like was to be interrupted when he was listening to the radio or reading the newspaper, when he slept until late or when he took a nap after lunch. And as long as his slippers were set parallel to the foot of the bed, his coffee was nearly scalding, there weren't any fatty bits in the milk, the children didn't run through the house, the sofa pillows were arranged the right way, the windows were closed no later than four o'clock, no racket was made before seven in the morning, the radio was never too loud or too soft, the bathrooms smelled like eucalyptus and he never had to eat the same dish two meals running, he didn't ask too much.

All right.

That wasn't the entire truth.

It was nearly the entire truth.

The part of 'nearly' that Euridice didn't like to remember had to do with the ever-so-sad night when she'd disappointed her husband by being unable to stain the bedsheet. If Euridice could have buried that night in the backyard, she would have, together with some chicken bones, which a neighbor had told her were good for the plants. Except that Antenor never allowed her to, and never allowed her to because of the Nights of Whiskey and Weeping.

Such nights occurred every two or three months. Antenor would arrive at home, kiss his wife on the forehead, go to change his clothes in the bedroom, and come back to the living room in his slippers. When Euridice and Cecilia began to set the dinner table, he would say: 'Today I'm going to eat a bit later, woman. First, I'm going to have my whiskey.'

Euridice would shoot him a look that said *You know what happens when you drink your whiskey*, and Antenor would respond with a look that said *I know what I'm doing when I drink my whiskey*.

The truth is that during the Nights of Whiskey and Weeping the only thing Antenor knew he was doing was drinking whiskey. After the first few sips, strange things began to happen, and Antenor saw no other alternative than to take a stand against them.

For example: at the beginning of these nights, everything seemed to be just fine. Antenor was Antenor, Euridice was Euridice, and Afonso and Cecilia were two happy children who played catchball in the living room. Metamorphoses took place after the first glass, because Euridice – who rushed to put the kids to bed early – walked out of the living room as Euridice and upon her return became *That slut who couldn't save herself for her husband on their wedding night*.

'Who was he?'

With his body sunk into the armchair, a glass of whiskey in his hand, Antenor gazed at his wife like a man who'd been stabbed in the heart. It was no use asking, 'Who do you mean, Antenor?'

'Him, Euridice. The guy. I have the right to know his name!'

How Antenor suffered. He wept until his nose began to run. He was overcome with self-pity. He was a hard-working man, a serious man, who didn't deserve to be married to a slut.

The metamorphoses continued. Afonso and Cecilia were no longer Antenor's children but the children of God knows who, because a woman who hadn't been chaste before marriage could very well continue to be unchaste – was that what a man like him deserved? Was it? 'Tell me, Euridice, is that what I deserve? Why? Why?'

The only upside to these nights was that they never took long to fizzle out. They always ended with Antenor asleep on the sofa and Euridice taking the glass of whiskey from his hand, whispering: 'Antenor, it's this whiskey you drink that makes me unchaste.'

Yes, Antenor was a good husband. That's what Euridice thought after the Night of the Great Feast, which turned into the Night of the Notebook Covered in Pavé. She usually regained her composure after convincing herself of her husband's qualities, but not that night. Antenor's burst of laughter wouldn't allow her to sleep.

When the living-room clock struck three, she understood it was a summons. She got up, put on her slippers, walked to the kitchen and went through the trash. The notebook was covered in leftover pavé; a clump of papers made sticky by the whipped cream. The dampness had muddied the words on some pages, making it difficult to follow the steps of certain recipes. It was impossible, for example, to read the recipe for the chocolate truffles. But Euridice didn't mind; she knew this recipe by heart. She had tried it for the first time at Cecilia's first birthday party. After that, all the women on the block asked for the recipe, and soon Euridice's sweet was making appearances at all the children's birthday parties in Tijuca. But what did it matter whether she could see the recipe or not? She wasn't even sure why she'd decided to rescue the notebook. Euridice pushed away her thoughts as she cleaned the cover of her black notebook with a rag. She stuck sheets of white office paper between the damp pages and stashed the book behind some encyclopedia volumes on the living-room shelf.

She walked back to the bedroom, and only then did she fall asleep.

Life went on. For the children, bananas and spaghetti. For her husband, food free of the texture of onions. For Euridice, chores that came to an end before they should, giving her time to sit on the sofa and admire her fingernail polish.

The months that followed the notebook's burial behind the encyclopedia volumes were not easy. She tried to dedicate herself to her children, but this was a cross-eyed sort of dedication. With one eye she made sure Afonso and Cecilia were dressed for school, and with the other she asked: *Can this really be all there is to life?* With one eye she helped the children with their homework, and with the other asked: *And when they no longer need me?* With one eye she told the children stories, and with the other asked: *Is there life beyond school uniforms, memorizing times tables and all these fables?*

What helped her to withstand it all were the soap operas on the radio. Every day at three in the afternoon, Euridice sat in the armchair next to the radio, pressed its buttons, and stared at the bookshelf that stretched along an entire wall of the living room. Her eyes wandered across the spines, and beside the spines she saw Frederico and Armando, two friends who fell for a farmer's daughter. She saw Betina, the mysterious woman who lost her memory and was found unconscious on the beach by a fisherman. She saw Maria Helena, so young, so single, and with child.

Euridice wrung her hands, wringing them for each character, her eyes fixed on the bookshelf – *No, Armando, please, don't kill Frederico! He's your brother. Betina, don't kiss Ricardo, he's the one who killed your mother! Maria Helena, your son will conquer the world, don't worry! Mama Dolores will make a great doctor of him.* Things were going on inside that little brown box, and nothing was ever going on in the life of Euridice Gusmao.

Life became even more eventless after the Gusmao-Campelo family acquired one of those marvels of that time and still to this day – a house maid. Maria das Dores arrived just in time to serve breakfast and left after washing the very last dinner plate, leaving behind her a trail of tidy beds, waxed floors, and sparkling bathrooms. Euridice continued to make trips to the market, the corner grocer, the butcher and the poultry shop, and to use any other excuse to get out of the house, as long as she could make it back at three in the afternoon to turn on the radio, wring her hands, and stare at the bookshelf.

The radio soap operas distracted Euridice for a while, but not for long. After a few months, the young woman would turn on the radio and stare at the bookshelf, but she no longer pondered whether Rita should marry Paulo or Ricardo, but instead, thought about the meaning of life.

She became taciturn. Every once in a while, she even gave a cross response to her husband.

'Euridice, I see there are some little bits of curdled milk in my coffee.'

'If you drank your coffee, you'd no longer see them.'

Maria das Dores – whose very name, Dores, meant suffering and destined her for a life of misfortune – only found her hardships multiplied. Euridice always found wrinkles in the bedspread, streaks on the floor and hairs in the shower. Maria didn't mind arriving at work at seven in the morning and leaving at eight at night, she didn't mind eating the same rice, beans, and stew every day, she didn't mind ironing linen shirts in the tiny room in the back of the house, which in the summertime reached temperatures resembling high noon on the equator, as long as she could make it home every night to see her little ones. Maria was the single mother of three children, who ate the food she left in the oven and played with the toys she left out for them, and were old enough to take care of themselves at home, it no longer being necessary to chain them to the bed to make sure they didn't get into the knife drawer or play with the stove.

But this isn't the story of Maria das Dores. Maria das Dores only makes occasional appearances, to wash the dishes or make up the beds. This is the story of Euridice Gusmao, the woman who could have been.

CHAPTER 3

Euridice was in need of a new project. She needed something to fill the morning hours of idleness and the afternoon hours of anguish, when the children were still at school. When everything appeared not only slightly maddening, everything was hopelessly maddening. In these empty hours she could feel her solitude transform into anguish, her anguish transform into madness, and this madness whispering to her: *One day I'll get you, one day yet I'll get you.*

One Friday, after slamming the door shut on her way out of the house to clear her head (*Maria does everything wrong, Maria is an idiot, she stained the towel, burned those pants, broke a glass, lost my earrings*), Euridice found herself walking towards Ravishing Coiffeurs. It had been more than two weeks since she'd had her hair done, and a good wife ought to always take care of herself for her husband, or else her husband might leave the house in search of that which he didn't find at home (curly hair, red nail polish and everything that was to be found between the strands of these curls and the toenails coated with polish).

Seated beneath the plastic mushrooms that housed the hair of Tijuca's upper-class women, Euridice leafed distractedly through the *Young Ladies' Journal*. This time she spent longer than normal on the sewing column. It gave directions for making a dress, with detailed explanations over twenty-three steps. She would need to measure the model, cut the pattern, stitch by hand and by sewing machine, do a fitting, do another fitting, fasten the buttons, sew the buttonholes, finish it off with some ruffles and – would you look at that – it was exactly such a dress that Euridice wanted, not because it was pretty or even because it was a dress, but because it involved a nine-piece pattern and twenty-three steps of something she'd never done before.

The process of convincing Antenor to buy a sewing machine lasted four days. The first time, he said no. The second time, he said no. The next time, another no. And then he said, 'Don't start on this business of sewing again, I can't stand this lament anymore. If it means I'll have peace again, then buy the damn thing, woman!'

Euridice had learned one of the oldest techniques in feminine guerrilla warfare: to repeat the request until the man gives his consent.

The next day she put on a dress and went downtown to buy her Singer sewing machine. It was tight, her dress, but she didn't notice. It was a Monday, the day for her to diet, and the truth is that in the weeks that followed Euridice was so engaged in learning sewing-ese that she would forget to eat, and forget to torment Maria. But she didn't forget her children, she attentively got them ready for school, greeted them with a big smile when they came home in the afternoon, cheerfully helped them with their homework, and asked Cecilia if she didn't want a new apron, if Afonso wouldn't like another pair of blue pants, and while Antenor watched the news on his recently acquired TV, Euridice cut the tracing paper for the pattern, added pleats, stitched hems, sewed on zippers, and gave herself entirely to the zigzag of the sewing machine, which to her sounded like music. If there were lyrics to this song, they would sing of hands at work, minds at rest, success and peace.

Now, this wasn't exactly what Zélia heard with her sharp ears, which she stuck up against the wall that joined the two houses. The zigzag of the sewing machine was the same, but Zélia gleaned a different message from the *tack-tack-tack*. What could bring a housewife accustomed to visiting the elegant Casa Sloper department store, to buying clothes for her husband at Casa José Silva and for her children at Bonita, what could bring the wife of a big-shot employee of the Bank of Brazil to spend her evenings and, at times, entire nights (Zélia could hear every, absolutely every sound that came from the house) bent over a sewing machine?

Poor woman, she was! The *tack-tack-tack* proved what Zélia already knew: the couple next door was not in a good financial situation, and Euridice found herself in the

unenviable position of sewing her own clothes. Those sump-
tuous dinners, those fancy home appliances, it was all an
illusion. If Antenor were the first on the block to have a
TV, he would also be the first to no longer have one. The
Gusmao-Campelos simply could not continue to spend
like that.

The next day the women on the block bemoaned the fact
that Euridice and Antenor were in financial straits. Some
of them placed bets that Maria das Dores wouldn't make
it through the month with a job. Others suggested that the
maid only stuck around on account of the meals. *Many of
them have no use for a salary, since they wouldn't know how to
spend it anyway*. Not to mention the other expenses. The
tuition for the children's schooling was most certainly late,
it was possible that Cecilia and Afonso would have to switch
to public school. They would have to buy their groceries on
credit, and would never again set foot in the upscale doctors'
offices downtown.

But the family's financial troubles existed only in the heads
of others, and had nothing to do with Euridice's deep desire
to continue her projects. They were good, those months.
The children arrived from school to a Euridice whose eyes
were full of enthusiasm and whose heart was open.

'What did you learn today at school?'

Afonso would tell her about amphibians, and Cecilia
about the planets.

'Mama, there are nine planets that orbit the Sun, and
the Earth is the third in line. If it were any closer to the

Sun, the Earth would be so hot that nobody could survive, and if it were further away it would be too cold and we'd all die.'

'And the Moon,' Euridice would reply, 'did you know that the Moon orbits the Earth, and that there are many moons throughout the universe?'

Cecilia's eyes grew wide with excitement and Afonso's did the same because he saw his sister doing it. Euridice climbed on to the stool and grabbed the encyclopedia volume about planets from the top of the bookshelf to explain the origin of the universe, the position of the stars, and the many suns far from Earth. She was such a good teacher that Cecilia soon knew more than all of her classmates, and Afonso learned about the planets long before any of his friends.

Euridice later sought out the encyclopedia volume with articles on amphibians and photos of brightly colored frogs explaining that those animals breathed not only through their noses but through their skin, and wasn't that fascinating, because we only breathe through our noses and mouths, and when we breathe in the air, it enters our lungs as oxygen and leaves as carbon dioxide. The two of them would learn this later in school, but perhaps they could speed things up a bit; they would see what the encyclopedia had to say. Euridice stepped up on to the stool again and grabbed the volume about the human body, and those afternoon hours passed before anyone noticed. Euridice with a book in her lap, her children on either side of her, the clock striking on the hour without anyone paying attention.

Antenor would arrive from work and kiss his wife on the forehead. He changed his clothes in the bedroom and walked back to the living room in his slippers. The family came together to eat the dinners that now appeared and disappeared from the table thanks to Maria, the quiet woman who kept mainly to the kitchen.

Antenor asked Afonso and Cecilia about school and they told him all about planets and amphibians. He promised to take them that Saturday to the Tijuca Forest, to catch tadpoles at the lake. 'That way, the two of you can see the kids of these amphibians up close.' The children jumped up and down with joy and told the news to Euridice, who was sewing at the other end of the sofa. Euridice smiled without looking up from her work and remained focused on each stitch when Antenor took the children to the garden to show them the Southern Cross, Venus, and maybe even the constellation Scorpius.

As soon as they returned home from one of their outings, the children would put on their pajamas and wait in bed for their father to read them stories by Monteiro Lobato. 'Where did we leave off?' 'Chapter Six of *The Twelve Labors of Hercules*, Papa.' 'That's right.' Antenor would read four or five pages before Afonso fell asleep, and the moment he got up, Cecilia would say, 'Just one more page, Papa, I want to know more about the centaurs.' Antenor would read a few more pages until Cecilia began to yawn. It was good to see his daughter taking an interest. He wanted her to complete her studies and, who knows, go to college. And make a good marriage. He would then give a kiss to each of the children and get ready for bed, as the next day would be packed with meetings.

Half an hour later, the entire house would be filled with silence and darkness, apart from the tiny lamp atop the Singer sewing machine belonging to Euridice Gusmao and the soft beat of her backstitch. Euridice sewed until she was exhausted, before falling into a sleep that was free of dreams, because she no longer needed them.

Some months later Euridice was once again overcome with restlessness. She could no longer whip up clothing for the children or new uniforms for Maria, towels for the side tables, or shirts for Antenor. She was in need of new projects, which would not be difficult to arrange. Euridice lived at a time when there were fewer stores than there are today, and on a street that was full of women – two crucial factors in the success of her endeavor.

On the day Euridice went out in search of clients, pity fell over Tijuca. They were sorry to see such a well-dressed woman hitting the streets in search of work. Euridice no longer had just one dress for going out, but seven or eight, or nine or ten. She had one for each day of the week, and another still because she found polka dots beautiful, and yet another because the checkered linen was on sale.

There came Euridice walking up the street, in a red dress with a flared skirt. A dress that before would have taken up the entire sidewalk but that now occupied a very discreet bit of space, since during those months of sewing she had lost two of her chins and many dress sizes, in part because she often thought of work to the detriment of eating and in part because she thought of how beautiful she would be inside that fitted suit.

'I can make any of the dresses found in the *Young Ladies' Journal* or *Radio Magazine*. I need only see the sketch to copy it down. You can buy the fabric yourself, miss, or I can buy it, the choice is yours.'

'Very well,' her client would say, eyes full of relief that she didn't find herself in Euridice's situation. A relief that inspired generosity and prompted the reply, 'Make this model here for me. You can buy the fabric yourself, just add it to my bill. If you need me to put down a deposit, let me know and I'll pay right now.'

Zélia also ordered a dress of her own, not out of necessity or pity for Euridice, but because she wanted to attend fittings at one of the most interesting places in all of Tijuca: her neighbor's living room. A place in which Zélia had never set foot, but would now be able to stick her nose because she'd been summoned.

On the days she had fittings for her particularly intricate dress, Zélia fixed her eyes on everything but the garment. The imperial-style, Brazilian-walnut crystal cabinet with five rows of a dozen Bohemian crystal glasses for red wine, white wine, whiskey, champagne and liqueurs; the Provençal buffet with its three drawers and gold-plated steel tongs; the Marie Thérèse chandelier with twenty-four lamps, twelve arms, and thirty-six crystal pendants; the cherrywood table with the glass top and eight matching chairs (one of them, Zélia noted, with a chipped foot); the serving plate with two wrought-silver serving trays, the two rectangular Persian rugs with varied tones of burgundy and beige; and all the marvelous gadgets that Antenor made a point of acquiring the minute they entered the stores because he considered himself to be a man ahead of his time: the radio with its case and toothpick legs, the tiny record player that fit in one of the corners of the bookshelf, the tall floor fan, the television in yet another case with toothpick legs, which, Zélia noted, varied slightly in tone from that of the radio, bringing a certain disharmony to the decor.

Zélia was just one of Euridice's many clients. The doorbell rang all the time, with women turning up to try on dresses. Maria spent her day making more coffee than one of the local coffee shops that served breakfast. The clinking of the demitasses mixed with the buzz of the clients, because a fitting session was never simply a fitting session. It was a fitting and a question about the children's school, a fitting and a complaint about the prices at the market, a fitting and a catching-up on the entire neighborhood.

More projects came Euridice's way. Rumors spread throughout the neighborhood that a certain good family woman needing to supplement the household income accepted special orders in her workshop. For the third time in a month, Euridice had to go to the stationery store to buy a notebook to write down her clients' measurements and requests. The best month of all Antonio's life. The bachelor's days were divided between selling paper supplies and resting from selling paper supplies, which he did in the apartment he shared with his mother, Dona Eulália. He would walk inside the house to hear his mother complaining of some ailment or remembering the good times when her family had money. Eulália spoke so much that perhaps it would be more correct to divide Antonio's hours between listening to his mother and resting from listening to his mother, which he passed selling paper supplies.

Euridice also increased her visits to fabric stores on the Rua Buenos Aires. One client wanted this fabric, the other wanted that fabric, yet another ordered a skirt on the very day she had returned from downtown with meters of linen and chiffon. So she went back to the stores and the stacks of textiles. She would greet the salespeople and the other clients, and ask if the woman behind the cash register had gotten over her flu. Later she focused on the counters, in search of special promotions.

On one such afternoon, lost amid the textiles, Euridice didn't notice the young woman next to her, leaning up against a pillar. She had a pained expression on her face and her right hand clasped the medallion buried in her bosom. It would take only one more step for this young woman to make her presence known. Just one more step, which she never took.

Euridice remained caught up in her own world, checking measurements in her little notebook and requesting lengths of fabric from the salesman. She walked to the cash register, paid for the fabric, and went home in a state of pensiveness. She was worried about her projects and deadlines. Afternoons and late nights weren't enough to take care of all the work she had before her. The solution would be to hire someone to help, and that's how Euridice came to hire a seamstress named Maricotinha.

Dona Maricotinha used cat-eye glasses and wore her hair swirled across her forehead. Her lips were puckered in such a way that they never moved, and she had been born with her arms crossed. Most of her sentences began with a 'but', and only problems came out of her mouth. ('But Miss, if you want to place the buttons here the dress isn't going to sit well' or 'But Miss, if you make the hem any narrower, the skirt is going to lose movement.')

Here, the reader must be wondering: Is every woman in this story sad or embittered? Not at all. Some of Euridice's acquaintances were luckier. Isaltina enjoyed needlepoint and had the privilege of laughing with her perfect teeth, something she did with some regularity since she had a husband with whom she enjoyed conversing and who had the money for dentist visits. Margarida had become a widow and was very happy because God had taken her husband but left her a pension, and what a relief that the opposite hadn't occurred. Celina never married but had received a hefty inheritance. She also had a good friend, whom she saw on Wednesdays and Fridays.

Dona Maricotinha, meanwhile, found nothing in life to be thankful for. She thought life was absurd. It was absurd to have to work as a seamstress beyond fifty years of age.

The blame belonged to her husband, to whom she had never given permission to die of emphysema but who had decided to do so anyway.

Near the beginning of June, the first gusts of winter wind blew through the streets of Tijuca. One of them hit Antenor, who had just left the shower naked to grab a new tin of talcum powder from the bedroom. Had Antenor discontinued the habit of applying talcum powder to his private parts at the same time other mortals had done so, the events that followed would never have taken place. But it was cold, the talcum powder in the bathroom was empty and Antenor liked to give a bit of a finish to his privates, so he left the bathroom dressed the same way he had come into the world. During this short walk, a cold wind hit him in the neck and traveled down his spine, causing him to shudder, which caused him to sneeze, and then caused Antenor to think he was becoming sick.

The next day he dragged his feet to work and dragged them back home. The day after, he only managed to drag his feet to the bathroom and then back to bed. That was all he could do. Even when Euridice brought him hot tea, even when she brought him chicken soup, even when she brought him another hot tea and another round of chicken soup.

That afternoon, Antenor's fever refused to break. During the hours of delirium, he missed the trolley to work and the deadline to finish a project. He missed the due date for the electric bill and was soon missing his pants. Now the house was dark, and all the neighbors stood before his naked body like a gang of judges. He didn't lose his kids, but his kids lost all reason, because they didn't do their homework and were held back a year in school as a result. *Euridice – where are you, Euridice? It was Euridice who let all this happen. Why didn't she tell me the trolley was passing by, that I needed to finish the project? Where was she when she should have been telling me to pay the bills and throw on some pants? Why didn't she look over our children's shoulders until they finished their homework? Now they're going to cut the electricity and fire me too. All because of that woman, the neighbors are going to repeat in unison: failure, failure, failure.* And he whispered to himself: *slut, slut, slut.*

His high fever continued and the doctor thought Antenor was suffering from pneumonia. He prescribed antibiotics and aspirin, and showed Euridice how to replace the cold towel on Antenor's forehead every twenty minutes. From that afternoon through to the next morning, Euridice switched the cold towel fifty-four times, and if it wasn't the cold towels that led to Antenor's recovery it was Euridice and her hands, which remained on her husband's forehead or in prayer position the entire night.

Antenor opened his eyes the next morning. It was a relief to know he hadn't missed his trolley or his deadline, and his pants were hanging in the closet. The children were at school and his wife was at his side. Euridice was not a slut, after all. Euridice gave meaning to all the parts of his life that, without her, would be undone. And it was then, at that moment, that Antenor loved his wife more than at any other moment. It would be good to be able to believe that

Euridice was telling the truth about their wedding night or – better still – believe that it didn't matter. But Antenor could not. He simply could not.

That morning Antenor remained in bed. He fell asleep and woke up a few times, and accepted the chicken soup, the hot tea, and his wife's care. The window overlooking the street remained half-open and it was nice to nap to the sounds of the street in the middle of the week, sounds unfamiliar to him: the pot-and-pan salesman offering his wares, the baker selling buns, the knife sharpener grinding knives.

After lunch, Antenor listened to other noises throughout the house. Women talking, coming in and out – he had no idea that Euridice had so many friends. And how was it possible to hear the sound of the sewing machine when Euridice's voice was coming from the other corner of the room? It was all very strange. Antenor got up from the bed and walked towards the living room without dragging his feet, already feeling better.

It was the shock of the scene before him that restored him to health.

In front of the mirror was Zélia, dressed only from the waist down and inspecting the pieces in the crystal cabinet, while Euridice marked the hemline of her neighbor's skirt with pins. Another woman, dressed only from the waist up, was having her measurements taken by an older, bespectacled seamstress. Two other ladies were drinking coffee and eating dry biscuits on the sofa. A black woman with nappy hair and a cheap cotton dress was working away on Euridice's sewing machine. The center table looked like the counter at a textile store on the Rua Buenos Aires. The Persian rug was covered in fabric scraps, pieces of thread and measuring tapes. On the dinner table were patterns cut in tracing paper, scissors, rulers, spools, and two sewing baskets.

'What is all this mess in my living room?'

Zélia cried out, one of the women spilled her coffee, and the other rushed to cover herself with scraps of fabric. Euridice looked at her husband and then at the floor.

'I'm making some dresses for my friends...'

Her explanation made no sense. Antenor would not give his support to that project, the transformation of his living room into a workshop, the transformation of his house into a circus, all that coming and going of women; it was worse than a doctor's office. And who was *that black woman* parked in front of the sewing machine?

'This is Damiana, she was recommended by Dona Maricotinha...'

'And who is Dona Maricotinha?'

Euridice thought it wise to confess everything at once. Dona Maricotinha was her assistant, and Damiana was an assistant to her assistant, because now she was sewing for women across the neighborhood and had no way to take care of all that work by herself. And you know how it is, besides the sewing, one needs to talk to the clients about patterns, take their measurements and carry out a fitting, and while she did one thing her assistants were doing others, so they could work at a faster pace.

Her rudimentary description of the production chain didn't please Antenor at all. While he listened, his nostrils flared until he looked like King Kong. At the same time, everyone in the room said they had to leave: the butcher's was going to close, it was going to rain, it was getting late. The only one left was *that black woman* with her eyes drilled into the side of the sewing machine, and she only stuck around because she needed that day's pay to buy her supper.

Euridice had been worried that Antenor might do that. During the days he was sick, she canceled her meetings with clients, but after the third day they showed up anyway. They had dances to go to, a dinner at the Tijuca Tennis Club or a party at the Club Bragança, and where else were they to get the scoop on the goings-on in households other than their own?

When everyone was in the room together, Euridice asked them to speak quietly, which they did not do. Then she began to think that Antenor could come down to join them, become acquainted with the project and think it was interesting, but she knew deep down that would never happen either.

During the months Euridice worked as the Most Talented and Affordable Seamstress in Tijuca (and Muda, Penha, and Vila Isabel), Antenor had remained aloof to his wife's productive ambitions. This time, Euridice had made use of another tactic of feminine guerrilla warfare: combat by omission (which keeps men from saying no).

She knew that at some point she would have to tell her husband about her plans, but his reproval was a given. She then thought about postponing the conversation until, who knows, the end of time.

In the early afternoon, the living room was transformed into a workshop, and shortly before five, Maria and Euridice would transform it back into a living room. Patterns, magazines, and fabrics vanished from sight, and if some scrap or other was left behind, it wouldn't be a big a deal. Antenor didn't pay attention to things at home. In Antenor's mind, there was a nearly tangible line drawn between his areas of the house and Euridice's. In the house they shared, he moved only through those spaces designated for him, never traveling beyond the route that consisted of bedroom–bathroom, bathroom–bedroom, couch–dinner table, dinner table–bedroom, bedroom–bathroom–kitchen table–hallway. Whatever existed beyond these limits was of no interest to him. Antenor's familiarity with the house was almost nonexistent. He had no idea what was in the refrigerator or the kitchen cabinets, much less the kitchen sink. He wasn't concerned with the contents of the credenza and only once in a while cast an eye over the bookshelf as though it were partly his, on account of the *Stories of Monteiro Lobato* he read to the children.

Everything else was everything else, and everything else was the domain of Euridice. Antenor was there to bring home a paycheck and to dirty plates and rumple the sheets, not to know how the clothes were laundered and the dinner made. As a result, he never discovered the endless meters of fabric stored in the credenza, or the pile of sewing magazines stuffed away in a drawer, or the fifty-seven patterns hidden behind the sofa. Seeing all this for the very first time, Antenor felt once again like a deceived husband, with the advantage that this time he was right.

When Antenor's nostrils could not grow any wider, *that black woman with nappy hair* thought it might be better to go hungry that night.

'Dona Euridice, I am going to take the dress on the ironing board to finish it at home.'

Antenor had never been so angry. The only reason he didn't throw the sewing machine, assistant and ironing board out the window was because he was worried about what others might say. It was also because he was worried others might say that he didn't want his wife sewing dresses for the neighborhood. They would think he was less of a man because his wife had to work.

The sewing machine and the assistant may not have flown through the window, but the neighbors had plenty to say about the yelling heard that night. Zélia had no need to put her ear against the wall to hear everything. *So I kill myself working at the bank for you to have the best of everything only to discover you're running a county fair at home?* But Antenor, I like working. *Your work is taking care of the house and the children.* But I already do this, Antenor. *Oh yeah? And why is it you never make those turkey medallions for me, huh? The ones with that brown stuff on top.* Because you always said they made you burp after eating them. *Don't you start with the excuses, Euridice.* That's what you said, Antenor, you said that you didn't want to eat them anymore, that you couldn't eat anything with onion in it after five o'clock, not even if the onion was chopped into tiny pieces. *I need a wife who's dedicated to her family. It's your responsibility to give me the peace of mind to go out and bring home a living. Do you have any idea how difficult it is to work in the loan department?* No, I don't. You never talk about your work. *I don't talk about it because you wouldn't understand.* Don't look at me like that, Antenor, I'm a good wife. *A good wife doesn't go looking for side projects. A good wife doesn't worry about anything but her husband and their children. I need peace to be able to work, you need to take care of the children.*

And then something interesting happened. Antenor couldn't stop repeating the same phrases over and over. 'Did you hear me, Euridice, did you hear me? I go out and work, you take care of the children. You hear, Euridice, you hear? I go out to work and you take care of the children.' He didn't even wait for his wife to say that she'd heard him. He simply began to repeat the phrase again, and again. 'I go out to work, you take care of the children.'

When Antenor managed to stop repeating himself, something stranger still occurred: with each new round of yelling, the children's problems multiplied. Cecilia had dirt beneath her fingernails, Afonso's hair was too long. Their noses were always running – a lot, they never stopped. Green, yellow, purple snot. They hadn't had a decent meal in weeks, don't think he hadn't noticed. Those poor kids only ate cornflour rolls. Cornflour rolls! And that was when they actually ate. They were children whose lives were thrown to the mercy of God, delivered to the fortune of Providence. Soon people would confuse them with street children.

CHAPTER 4

We haven't yet mentioned someone who has played an important role in Euridice's life since the very beginning. We're talking about the Side of Euridice that Didn't Want Euridice to Be Euridice.

The Side of Euridice that Didn't Want Euridice to Be Euridice had tormented her since her school years. At that time she still thought the world was a beautiful and interesting place, with its numbers, letters, and infinite combinations of letters and numbers. She developed an intimacy with words long before her classmates. By the first grade she always left the house informed, after reading the back of the newspaper that hid her father's face. Euridice's mother, Dona Ana, saw a future in her daughter's progress.

'Very soon this girl will be able to help us at the greengrocer's.'

Euridice's teacher, Clara, was a sweet young woman. She would smile when her students gave a correct response and would smile when they were wrong. As a result, everyone wanted to give the correct response but no one was afraid to be wrong. Clara was never seen wearing anything but a blue skirt and white shirt, or with any expression on her face other than a smile. Her clothes smelled of coconut soap, everything about her smelled of coconut soap. Each day after class she washed her shirt and set it out to dry. She also washed shirts that weren't hers, which her mother then ironed and returned to the mansions of Rio Comprido. One cloudy and chilly day, Clara insisted on wearing the uniform, even if it was a little damp. First she caught a cold, then she developed the flu. She later died of pneumonia, and except for the good she did for her students over the course of three years, she had passed through the world unnoticed.

Her replacement was Dona Josefa, a woman who would live on forever in her pupils' nightmares. No one prepared students better for life beyond the classroom. Dona Josefa taught them the rudiments of sarcasm and hierarchy. She developed obsessive-compulsive personalities among her pupils through sentence repetition that filled countless note-books, afternoons, and the aforementioned nightmares. *I will not arrive late to class*, one student wrote for an entire hour after lunch, even if the following day he would once again arrive late, since the line for the bathroom in his tenement house during the early morning hours was comparable to that of Central Station at the end of the afternoon, and since he was only a boy it fell to him to be the last in line.

It took a while for Dona Josefa to impress her pedagogical methods on the young Euridice. She couldn't criticize the homework that was completed with great accuracy, or the aced exams. She also couldn't ignore that irritating little hand that shot up all the time, either to ask a question or give an answer. She discovered how to proceed during the third week of school. It was the last class of the morning and the students were copying a text by Camões from the chalkboard. Euridice had already finished copying the paragraph. She asked permission to speak.

'Teafer. I haulf to ufe the bafloom.'

'What?'

'I haulf to ufe the bafloom, teafer.'

Dona Josefa didn't respond. She stood up from the desk and walked from one side of the room to the other. The best way to discipline Euridice was suddenly right there in front of her eyes.

'I didn't understand what you said.'

'The bafloom, teather.'

Dona Josefa stopped, raised her hand to her chin, and squinted.

'This word, bafloom... I've never heard it.'

The entire class burst out laughing. Euridice felt a knot in her stomach, something she'd never felt before. It rose up through her gullet, passed to her throat, and paralyzed her tongue.

'I ne... I nee... I nee... I need... to go.'

That day, Euridice was only allowed to go to the bathroom if she learned how to pronounce her 'THs', her 'Rs' and her 'Ss'. She peed at her desk, and felt the warm urine slowly grow cold. She had to remain at school until the middle of the afternoon so she could write 'I need to use the bathroom' on the chalkboard two hundred times. For the rest of the year she still had to use the bafloom but was able to avoid the girl's room at school. She stopped drinking water after six in the evening and refused to drink milk with breakfast. It was a good strategy. On many days, Euridice had to control her bladder until long after the end of classes as she spent more than an hour and a half writing on the chalkboard that the man who discovered BRaSil was PedRo ALVarez CabRal, and that the correct names of the Amazon River tributaries were PuRús, NegRo, MadeiRa, and JapuRá.

Leaning against the desk on the little stage at the front of the classroom, with Euridice's perfect exam in her hands, Dona Josefa wrested laughs out of Euridice's classmates.

'You think you're smart? Then repeat after me: Dom PedRo pRoclaimed THe founding of THe Republic in the PRaça da Aclamação.'

It didn't take long for Euridice to understand that it would have been better if Dom Pedro II hadn't founded the republic. Better if it had been Dom João or Columbus. The girl learned to smatter her tests and homework with mistakes, to escape Dona Josefa's rage. That's how the Side of Euridice that Didn't Want Euridice to Be Euridice was born.

When the Side of Euridice that Didn't Want Euridice to Be Euridice was already quite developed, Dona Josefa left the girl alone. It was more or less around this time that Euridice learned to say pRoblem and pRejudice correctly, forgot the puRsuit of knowledge, and understood that the world was a pRecaRious place. Euridice had learned about the distorted notion of pRogress that people have. She understood exactly where this pRogress of BRazil's would lead.

Dona Josefa's contribution to this split existence of Euridice's was reinforced in the autumn of 1943. Euridice was turning fourteen, and, that January at least, everything seemed promising. The weekly open-air market that had been held one block from the greengrocer's moved a few blocks away. Local residents had no desire to walk up and down more hilly streets, and business at the store picked up. Senhor Manuel was so excited with the unexpected increase in profits that he bought Euridice and her sister Guida gold chains with medallions of Our Lady of Fátima.

'Here is a piece of jewelry to be part of your trousseau,' their father said, somewhat awkwardly.

The two little boxes lined with white satin seemed to be gleaming, as they lit up the faces of the young girls who opened them. Euridice and Guida hugged their father, and then left the stiff man in the living room to have a look at themselves in their mother's dressing table. They felt special, as though the qualities of the necklaces had extended to them.

'Wait a sec, something's missing,' Guida said, and ran to the bathroom. She returned with red lipstick, which she applied to her puckered lips.

'I want some, too,' said Euridice.

'You're still very young to use lipstick.'

'But I want to.'

'So, then go like this with your lips.'

Euridice imitated her sister. After applying the lipstick to Euridice, Guida made a mark on each cheek. She spread the red line around with her hands.

'Now we're talking. You look like an actress!'

Euridice opened her eyes wide and looked into the mirror.

'Make my hair look just like yours, Guida.'

Guida walked over to the closet and returned with curlers and pins. She began to style her sister's hair as though she knew exactly where each strand should fall. The strands were transformed into brunette waves that fell across the girl's shoulders.

'Where did you learn to do hair like this?'

'Around…'

'Around where?'

'Around, Euridice.'

It hadn't been long since their mother had decided to allow Guida to go to the cinema with her friends, which the young girl did not only to watch films but to admire hairdos and dresses, those of the movie stars and those of the audience. Guida was unable to change her dress each time since she only had one outfit for going out. But her hair – this she could do up however she wished, and do it differently each time.

Euridice truly believed her sister had the authority to do all of these things. In her imagination, the *around* Guida spoke of was a place of exotic locales, interesting people and different experiences. This *around* was home to everything that existed beyond the walls of the school and the greengrocer's, the only world Euridice knew.

On the afternoon their father gave them the necklaces, the two girls spent hours in front of their mother's dressing table. Guida felt too old to be doing her sister's hair, Euridice felt older for doing the same things as her sister. They didn't notice the March breeze rustling the curtains, or the dog barking in the distance. They didn't hear the trolley coming down the street, or the song of the neighbor's canaries.

Senhor Manuel felt like a rich man. The man who had melted his deceased father's gold tooth to make his wedding rings was now able to support his family and please his progeny. He permitted himself the luxury of spoiling his daughters, providing them with after-school activities. He spoke with Jean Luc, the confirmed bachelor who lived at the end of the street with five cats (according to the latest count) and gave classes in French and music. Guida chose French and Euridice decided to learn the recorder.

Guida didn't make it through the first month of classes. The verb conjugations induced wrinkles on her smooth forehead. How was it possible to combine the letters of the alphabet in so many unfamiliar ways? She soon declared that the French classes were interfering with her performance in school and buried her textbook deep in the bookshelf. She resumed spending long afternoons seated on the sofa, reading novels from the *Young Ladies' Library* or leafing through women's magazines.

Euridice asked her parents to use the money left over from Guida's French lessons to pay Jean Luc so that she could have extra classes. She also practiced an hour per day during the week and two hours each Saturday and Sunday. It wasn't long before the musical exercises became cantatas and sonatas, and the cantatas and sonatas ethereal poetry that lifted the moods of everyone in Santa Teresa.

The recorder was Euridice's first love. When she arrived home, she would do her homework, taking care to insert the occasional mistake to please Dona Josefa, and then sit up straight in front of her sheet music. When it was announced that the school would be forming a choir, Euridice offered to provide accompaniment on the recorder, and after the choir director heard the young girl play, Dona Josefa had no way to argue against it. The next month, the famous composer Heitor Villa-Lobos showed up at the school to talk about the benefits of choral singing. Hearing Euridice play, he took the cigar from his mouth and proclaimed: 'I want this girl to join my conservatoire.'

Euridice jumped up and down, inside and out, but her parents said no, perhaps not, definitely not. The classes with

Senhor Jean Luc were going so well, what more did she need? As far as her parents were concerned, the recorder would never be an end in itself. The recorder was merely the means. The means to increase their daughter's talents so she could make a good marriage. The means to entertain the family after dinner, when one of them would ask: 'Play this little march.' Euridice didn't need classes with that eccentric composer.

'But I really, really want to,' the young girl protested, pursing her lips, crossing her arms, furrowing her brow, and pounding her fists against the bedroom door.

The following days saw unprecedented confrontations. Half of Euridice thought her parents were right, the other half thought they'd lost their minds to throw away an invitation from Villa-Lobos. The Side of Euridice that Didn't Want Euridice to Be Euridice bolstered her parents' arguments. How would she get to the conservatoire in Praia Vermelha? Could the interaction with artists be a good thing for a young lady? It was risky. Music ought to be administered in the correct dosage, since a life without melody loses meaning and a life with too much melody could lead to excesses. Artists were people who led abnormal lives and were morally ambiguous, artists were 'those people.'

'Let me take the girl to the conservatoire!' Guida said.

'You can't go because we need you to help at the shop,' Senhor Manuel responded.

'I'll work a double shift on Saturday to take Euridice during the week.'

'What you want to know is if there are good-looking boys in this conservatoire. Euridice isn't going, and you certainly aren't either.'

Guida shrugged her shoulders, shot Euridice a look that said *I tried*, and went back to reading her magazine.

Theirs wasn't a house with much room for discussion. Dona Ana and Senhor Manuel could hear but could not listen. They were incapable of understanding anything that didn't interest them, and nothing that was different interested them. The most significant innovation in their lives was trading their tomato stand in Alvarães, Portugal, for a tomato stand on the Rua Almirante Alexandrino, in Rio. When faced with a novelty of some sort, the couple responded with some variation of *I haven't seen it and I don't like it, I don't know anything about it and I don't want to, I don't want it now and I won't want it later.* There was also the response that consisted simply of making a face and saying *Good Lord!* Having a daughter study with the greatest composer of the time was far beyond the understanding of those Portuguese immigrants. A strange man, who was never seen without a cigar in his mouth. *Good Lord!*

Euridice fought with her parents more during that time than at any other period of her entire life. She screamed at them, something she didn't even know she was capable of doing. How she wanted to study with Villa-Lobos! When she played the recorder she didn't feel compelled to make mistakes, she was able to create a perfect melody. Why couldn't life be like that, too? Why couldn't she do whatever she pleased, why couldn't she do everything she ever dreamed of, why couldn't she play until her fingers and her lips hurt? When she played, the only things that existed were her and the recorder; it was a perfect and tiny world.

She wanted it so badly that she had no problem playing this game of tug-of-war alone, with sporadic help from her sister, who every now and then lifted her eyes from her magazine to lend Euridice a hand. 'But Mama, Euridice could play in the symphony one day!' 'Quit it, Guida. Don't stick your nose where it doesn't belong.' Euridice tugged and tugged, even though she knew that her parents outweighed her on the other side.

At some point the two parties grew so exhausted that Euridice only managed to repeat *I want to,* and her parents' only response was *No.* Euridice responded with a *Why not?*, her parents responded with *Because.* In the end, it amounted to nothing more than a conversation between a bunch of crazy people who'd forgotten their entire vocabulary, one side asking *Why not?* and the other responding *Because. Why not? Because. Why not? Because.* Later, the whole drama, and all that distress, would disappear in a matter of seconds as a result of a single look.

It happened on a Thursday afternoon at the greengrocer's. Euridice and Dona Ana were at the cash register, facing opposite directions. The family lunch had been a chorus of *Why nots* and *becauses.* Around three o'clock, Dona Jovina walked in with her son José, looking for potatoes. A word here, a word there (Dona Jovina was looking for potatoes, but also for some conversation), and the customer noticed the sour expressions of mother and daughter. She asked what had happened.

Dona Ana sighed deeply before revealing, with sad eyes, the endless musical debate that occupied the apartment atop their store. She left out the yelling, the broken glasses and all the nights when her daughter didn't touch her food, as part of a hunger strike that deepened her dimples and her determination to become a professional musician.

'That's just it, Dona Jovina, I've been telling Euridice that she shouldn't put her energy into a musical career. What she needs is to finish her studies and concentrate on the things girls of her age do. Playing with friends, meeting a boy, and eventually making a family.'

Dona Jovina nodded in agreement, while José shot Euridice a flirtatious look. The girl lowered her eyes. At that moment, Euridice learned that some gazes are different from others and that some are capable of changing us not simply within but without, as she was suddenly quite unable to sit comfortably in the chair. As the potatoes were chosen, paid for and packaged up, the girl remained unsettled, conscious of her new body, transformed by a gaze.

She didn't eat that night, but it wasn't because of the recorder. It was because of the young boy's flirting. From ten until two in the morning she kept thinking about the way José had gazed at her. From two o'clock until six the scene was replayed with the addition of long walks holding hands through the Campo de Santana, a marriage proposal on the

Largo dos Guimarães, dinners between the families and a honeymoon in Friburgo. Asleep or wide awake, Euridice thought of nothing else. Not even of her recorder, which hardly required much space.

When she woke the next day it was as if the dispute about the music classes had never happened. Who was Villa-Lobos? What was a recorder? The Side of Euridice that Didn't Want Euridice to be Euridice rejoiced; the other part said *OK, but this isn't over yet*. Euridice pinched her cheeks to turn them red, tried curling her hair like Guida, went to school happy as could be. She counted the hours until it was time to go home and nestle into the chair beside the cash register at the greengrocer's.

She thought about sharing her secret with her sister. Guida was one of those girls who are born knowing everything or, in her case, everything that was worth knowing about, which was not the same 'everything' that Euridice knew. Guida was never an exceptional student, and to that day, even having completed high school, she had to use her fingers to calculate bills at the store, which still provided no guarantee she would do it right. But she knew how to apply red nail polish to the nails of those fingers, and without smudges. Guida also knew how to speak to adults, and it was she who faced Dona Josefa, saying, 'If I catch you being cruel to my sister, I promise I will tell the principal everything.' It was because of Guida that Euridice resumed drinking water at night, and it was because of Guida that she relaxed enough to learn to pronounce her 'Rs'.

The two girls completed one another. When Euridice woke up in a cold sweat in the middle of the night, swearing that there was a ghost walking in the attic, it was Guida who held her hand and said, 'Don't worry, it's only a skunk and her children. It's the creaking of their footsteps you're hearing.' When Guida lost all hope, with head in her hands and elbows resting on a book, on account of all the microorganisms she needed to memorize for a test the following day, it was Euridice who stayed by her side, repeating, 'We'll find a way to remember them. Let's start with the protozoa, who have two types of skeletons and move using flagella or cilia.'

And when Euridice returned home from school in tears, telling her mother how she'd hurt herself, perhaps climbing aboard the trolley, it was Guida who took over the explanations, handing Euridice much more than the tiny towel Dona Ana gave her 'to stop the bleeding.'

'Listen here, Euridice, you didn't injure yourself. From here on out this is going to happen once a month. It means you're becoming a woman.'

Guida went beyond the call of sisterly duty and explained to Euridice the reason for this bleeding and what needed to occur to make a woman pregnant. Euridice's eyes opened wide at this insight into her sister's world. It was a place where strange things happened and where Guida was the wisest woman of all. Guida went above and beyond yet again. She embraced her sister and told her that one day she would become a beautiful woman, would find a good husband, have many children, and live in a house with a garden.

How did Guida know all that? She simply knew because she knew. Guida was one of those young women who are born knowing everything.

Guida also knew how to flirt. She even had experience in the stage that followed. One Sunday in April, shortly before the battles over the recorder, she informed her parents that a young man whom she held *in great esteem* would be coming to see her after lunch.

Marcos appeared as the bells of the Church of the Largo marked two o'clock and wasted no time creating a bad impression. Instead of extending his hand to Senhor Manuel he offered a sort of oriental greeting, holding his hat in place and making a bow of respect. That was the strangest greeting the Portuguese man had ever seen, but he bowed in return – perhaps it was the latest fashion among the youth of Rio. Marcos pretended he didn't see the older man's discomfort. It was better to invent some exotic form of greeting than to offer a sweaty hand to shake. During the entire visit, he only parted with his hat for a second, to timidly gesture to Euridice, who was pretending to read a book in the corner of the room. In the space of the next half-hour, Dona Ana and Senhor Manuel learned everything they needed to know about the young man with the reddened face.

'Do you work, young man?'

'I'm studying. Medicine.'

'Where do you live?'

'Botafogo.'

'And your father – what does he do?'

'He's chief of staff to the mayor.'

'And your mother, what's her name?'

'Mariana.'

'Do you have siblings?'

'Five of them.'

'And what are your intentions with our daughter?'

'The noblest possible.'

Perhaps as a result of their surprise at the news, perhaps as a result of Guida's sureness, perhaps because the interviewee lived in Botafogo and studied medicine, the courtship was accepted without drama or prohibition. Guida was allowed to accompany Marcos to the movies. The rest of the courtship was to take place on the sofa on Rua Almirante Alexandrino, with the lamp on one side and Dona Ana darning socks on the other.

Marcos was an especially tall, thin and refined boy. He was also responsible for the Sugarloaf Mountain that grew up between Guida and her family. After she met Marcos, after receiving the tenderness of those hands that had never known true labor and after feeling the gaze of those eyes that had never known worry, Guida began to live in a world much too sophisticated to put up with the others under her roof (an uneducated Portuguese couple and a girl with braids and hairy legs).

She began to lock herself in her bedroom. To eat meals separately from the others. And to consider family life as consisting only of leafing through the *Young Ladies' Journal* on the armchair in the corner of the living room.

'Open this door right now, Guida. Your father came home from work more than an hour ago and wants to see you.'

'I'll open it in a second. I'm finishing getting ready.'

'Open up right now.'

The silence that followed convinced Dona Ana that the door would never open.

'What sort of manners are these? Where have you ever seen such a thing? What did I do to deserve such rebels for daughters? Guida wants nothing to do with us and Euridice wants nothing but to complain about the recorder. It was different when I was a child – I'd get it if I treated my parents this way! But in this house one daughter doesn't ever respond to questions and the other has a response for everything.'

Afternoon arguments became the norm, and after a while Guida's parents grew accustomed to their daughter's distance. They convinced themselves that it was a phase, that there was nothing to worry about. They had one daughter here, another there, neither had become pregnant, so all they needed to worry about was selling tomatoes. It was Euridice who found her sister's silence disconcerting.

'Guida, want to know what happened today during recess?'

'Hmm…'

'Guida, want to teach me how to make this lemon face mask?'

'Hmm…'

'Guida, shall we do each other's hair?'

'Hmm…'

Guida wasn't in a very talkative phase, but even so Euridice tried to speak to her sister about José's flirting at the green-grocer's. *She's going to help me, for old times' sake,* the younger sister thought. Times which weren't that old at all, just a few months back, but which seemed more remote since Guida's silence had increased the distance between them. It was all Marcos's fault. At first, Euridice had found him handsome, but now she thought him ugly because she knew Guida spent all her time speaking to him. She must have spoken to Marcos so much that there were no words left over for her.

'Guida?'

'Hmm…'

'What are you reading?'

'Can't you see?'

'No.'

'Yes, you can. It's the *Young Ladies' Journal*.'

'But what are you reading? *Inside* the magazine.'

'It wouldn't interest you.'

'It does interest me, otherwise I wouldn't be asking.'

'It's a test. To find out if your boyfriend likes you a lot or just a little.'

'I want to take it.'

'You don't have a boyfriend.'

'But I want to take it.'

'I already told you, you don't have a boyfriend.'

'And why are you taking it? Do you think Marcos doesn't like you?'

'Stop being silly, Euridice. Go play your recorder.'

Euridice followed orders and went to grab her recorder. Less out of a desire to play and more because the recorder was right next to Guida, and that would give her an opportunity to pull her hair. Guida returned the favor by twisting Euridice's skin; Euridice defended herself by digging her nails into her sister's flesh. The two girls were still locked in battle when Dona Ana appeared, broke up the fight and sent them to their rooms.

'I've never seen the two of you fighting! And now that you're grown up I have to punish you both?'

The fight went some way to helping Euridice, who took advantage of the incident to cry out all the tears she'd been holding back since the beginning of the battle over her recorder. No one in that family understood her, no one wanted what was best for her, and even Guida, whom she could always talk to, no longer paid her any attention. But José, he would understand her. Euridice didn't need school, the recorder, or Guida. She only needed José.

She increased her hours helping out at the greengrocer's. She stole Guida's lipstick, making her lips redder than she should have. Euridice knew it was only a matter of time until she would see José again. He's going to show up, she thought, keeping an eye on the street and assisting customers with a patient smile.

José appeared towards the end of the week. Euridice sat up in her chair and felt an urgent need to face the cash register. There was José, there was that gaze of his.

Except that this time, the gaze was directed at another girl. José walked into the store with Odete, who lived a few blocks away. He helped the girl with her shopping, carefully selecting the fruit. He picked the best bananas, apples, and figs while Odete chose potatoes and onions. The two didn't even seem to notice there were other people around them and in reality there weren't, because as soon as they had finished paying, Euridice was reduced to a hand that gave them their change. José did glance at Euridice for a second, but only to say with his eyes: *About the other day, that was just a joke.* José and Odete walked out into their own world, leaving Euridice standing amid the damaged apples and split figs that had gone unchosen.

It hurt so badly that Euridice lost all desire to talk to her sister, read her books, or make mistakes in her homework. She looked like a wind-up doll, with lifeless eyes, an expressionless mouth, and a slouched body, fulfilling its obligations mechanically and silently. Euridice couldn't see beyond her own sadness, to the point that she forgot she even had a sister.

And to the point that she did not hear the stir that announced Guida's flight one Monday night. Euridice only snapped out of her daze upon hearing her mother's screams the next morning. 'My Guida has run away! My Guida has run away!' Dona Ana belted out, kneeling in front of her daughter's empty closets.

Seeing her mother struggle with Guida's flight, seeing her father embrace her mother in an attempt to absorb her sadness, seeing how her sister was not to be found in the corner of her bedroom or any other part of the house, Euridice felt as though her heart was being shoveled out of her chest. For her, running away was worse than dying. With death, or sudden death, at least, one leaves without knowing and without a chance to say goodbye. When running away, the person is fully aware they are going, but they don't bother to say farewell.

How had Euridice failed to notice that Guida was about to run away? Why hadn't she tried to talk to her sister? Why hadn't her sister tried to talk to her? Their parents had never forbidden her from seeing Marcos, and had even permitted her to go to the cinema with him, so why had Guida run away? Who would explain to her all the things she didn't know from that point on?

Euridice had no answers to these questions. She only had an answer for one thing: *Could Guida have left because of our fight?* She needed to find some logic to it all, she needed a definitive response, and she decided that yes, part of the reason for Guida's flight was their argument, so she shared much of the responsibility for her sister's disappearance.

The family wasn't sure what to do with Guida's bedroom. Dona Ana left the door closed, but later Senhor Manuel opened it because the closed door gave the impression their daughter was still there. The open door also caused discomfort, since it was possible to see the bookshelf that Guida had left empty when she took her *Young Ladies' Library* series with her. There was also the matter of the bed. Senhor Manuel thought the bed ought to be dismantled, but Dona Ana insisted on leaving the mattress there: what if Guida decided to show up again, where was she to sleep? It was decided that the bedroom door would remain open a crack. When Euridice walked through the hall, she craned her neck to keep an eye on the room, as though her sister might sprout forth from the mattress. Guida hadn't taken the magazines she used to read in the living room. They remained there for a while, as though they were an extension of the missing girl. No one looked through them, no one threw them away. One day a picture frame with her sister's photo appeared in the living room. Senhor Manuel and Euridice didn't need to ask who had placed it there.

At first, the family managed to cope with their sadness because they had hope. Each day, they waited for the post-man, as the letter Guida hadn't left when she ran away could very well show up in the mail. Twice a day, Senhor Manuel would run to the pharmacy to check whether his daughter had left a message via the only telephone in the neighborhood.

News from Guida never arrived, and the family stopped waiting. From that point on, Senhor Manuel and Dona Ana no longer cried, but were never again seen laughing. Euridice could see how vulnerable her parents were, and she wanted to protect them. She felt she needed to bring them twice the amount of happiness she had before. She promised never to fight again, never to exile herself from the family as Guida had done. She would be the best daughter of all, an exemplary girl, even if this girl were completely in tune with The Side of Euridice that Didn't Want Euridice to Be Euridice.

In one final attempt to discover Guida's whereabouts, Senhor Manuel went to the chief of staff's office at the city hall.

'Tell His Excellency that the father of his son Marcos's girlfriend is here.'

An hour and a half passed. The Portuguese man squeezed his cap, just as Marcos had done on the day they'd met. He looked straight ahead, resigned. Around lunchtime, a woman returned with a response.

'Senhor Godoy sent me to tell you that he has no son named Marcos.'

CHAPTER 5

Now that both sides of Euridice have been introduced, it's easy to understand why this woman takes one step forward then another step back. Why she begins projects but is then not able to stand up to her husband. Why she didn't tell Antenor to go fly a kite when he began laughing during the Night of the Grand Banquet. And why, on the day of the Legendary Fight Over the Sewing Workshop, which followed the Great Flu, Euridice didn't raise her voice to say *My hands are mine and mine alone and I'll do whatever I want with them, and I want to use them to sew dresses and to point my finger in your face and tell you that my hands are mine alone and I'll do whatever I damn well please with them.*

Euridice didn't use her hands to declare her independence, but to cover her downcast eyes. She knew that her husband was right, according to all that was good and reasonable, and according to the reasonable person she had promised to be after Guida ran away.

On the day of their fight in her workshop, Antenor's voice grew louder, and Euridice's softer. Her protests became weaker and weaker, and Zélia, who began listening in to the argument seated quite comfortably on her sofa, soon had to put her ear up against the wall to hear the last few words. Even so, she couldn't manage to make out how it all ended.

She didn't need to wait long to find out. Alleging health problems, Euridice announced that she was giving up sewing, passing her client list and unfinished orders off to Dona Maricotinha. The announcement led to protests on all sides, since the clients were worried about becoming voodoo dolls when the time came to try on clothes made by Dona Maricotinha alone, and Dona Maricotinha complained about so much extra responsibility. She would have to neglect her own clients to meet the demands of Euridice's. Dona Maricotinha left out that her many clients added up to a row of zeros. But she was sure to mention that the work would affect her blood pressure, and demanded payment worth two months' of Damiana's salary, to ensure they could complete all the orders.

Euridice didn't argue. The next day she showed up with the money, in a gesture so selfless that it made Dona Maricotinha regret not asking for more in exchange for neglecting her zero clients. The two women said goodbye, Euridice shut the door, and a pall fell over the Gusmao-Campelo household.

There was, of course, the creak of bathroom sinks and showerheads in the mornings. The whistle of the kettle declaring the hot water was ready for the coffee, the rustle of newspaper pages at the kitchen table. There was the echo of footsteps in the hallway, headed for school or to work. But none of these noises belonged to Euridice. The woman spent hours sitting and staring at the bookshelf in the living room. Maria grew worried. It had been more than a week since Euridice had told her the serving trays were dirty, the napkins were folded wrong, the orange juice was full of pulp, or that she had waited too long to slice the pineapple.

Cecilia and Afonso also noticed their mother's silence.

'Mama, look at the project I did about the Etruscans. See this part with the map? I copied it from the history book all on my own.'

'It's wonderful, son.'

'Mama, I finished reading Graciliano Ramos's *Barren Lives*. It's really a sad book.'

'You're right, it is, Cecilia.'

But Euridice didn't climb up on the stool to grab the encyclopedia and show Afonso the Etruscans' castles. She didn't climb up on the stool to grab the autographed copies of her Graciliano Ramos books, or tell Cecilia that *Anguish* was an even sadder story.

Euridice was a wife who knew how to behave. A woman dedicated to the home and to her children, and who now went to bed at the same time as her husband did, and didn't wake up early to entertain herself at the sewing machine.

A wife who sat quietly at his side as he watched TV, and offered him her forehead to kiss when he left the house and arrived home from work. She was everything Antenor had always wanted. Yes, everything he'd always wanted.

Or was she?

No, no she wasn't. He didn't want a Euridice like that. Seeing his wife in a constant state of apathy, Antenor understood that what he thought he'd always wanted wasn't what he really wanted. But what was it, then, that he wanted? He searched for answers during a night of insomnia. But insomnia and work at the bank didn't mix, so he stopped looking for answers. What he knew for certain is that for the first time in their married life they had a bigger problem than the incident on their wedding night.

Despite everything, or despite the nothingness that Euridice's life had become, Antenor was a good husband. The son of a civil servant and a poet who never published a book, he had grown up in a house of few meals and a lot of mess. The only structure in his family's life were the couplets and tercets his mother recited. *A kiss that is a glory and a torment, a soul in search of the firmament, the vows and caresses of one who blasphemes. The heart suffers to exasperation, an affection that is simple and sacred, a man requires love and in his arms your body delicate.* Maria Rita's life was a stage of private performances, and while that life may have been tedious it was much better than that of her audience, composed of the six children she'd given birth to before the age of twenty-five.

Feliciano would arrive from his government office in a state of wonder at his wife's abilities, the way she managed to leave the house in even greater chaos than it had been early that morning. The living-room floor was littered with dirty diapers, orange peel, wooden trucks, crawling kids and filthy bibs. The beds remained in a permanent state of *to be made*. The kitchen was overrun with cockroaches, crawling over the bits of food stuck to the dishes. Seated on the only armchair that hadn't been converted into a clothes hanger would be Maria Rita, wearing her oversized white camisole and holding a notebook of verses. Aside from her narrow eyes, the only thing she had inherited from her Tupi ancestors was a resistance to the rules of daily Western life.

The couple always began fighting at 5.45 in the afternoon.

'You don't understand, I'm a poet, an artist! A free spirit who has been chained to this life.'

'Maria Rita, I support your art, but this child has the rear of a baboon! And just look at our daughter's hair, we need to cut it right up to the nape of her neck, there's no way we'll untangle the knots now.'

Maria Rita would run to the bedroom to cry and her husband would be right behind to console her, since he couldn't resist her honey-colored curls and heart-shaped mouth. After a bit of squabbling, they'd make up and return to the living room to pick up the children and the orange peel. Perhaps out of habit, perhaps out of hopefulness, around seven o'clock Feliciano would ask what was for dinner.

'Bananas.'

Everyone knew that Maria Rita wasn't cut out for that life, and on the coldest day in August she decided that she wasn't cut out for any life at all. The misunderstood poet killed herself with rat poison. Perhaps her greatest contribution to her family was to lock herself in the bedroom, so that her children couldn't see her twisted body and her waxy face covered in white foam.

The tragedy on Rua das Marrecas was known in detail only to Feliciano, who, arriving from work, found nothing strange about the children scattered across the living room but did wonder about the boy pounding ceaselessly on the bedroom door. After breaking down the door, Feliciano used his hands to cover the eyes of young Antenor, who needed all of two seconds to witness the scene that would haunt him forever. He was six years old.

Two days later the Jornal do Commercio announced the death of Maria Rita, saying:

The intelligent poetess Maria Rita Campelo was befallen by an insidious and obscure disease, and after a long period of painful suffering left this earth at 1.20 in the afternoon of the nineteenth day of this month. She was buried yesterday in the Cemetery of São João Batista with an extraordinary number of attendees, men, women, and children of all rungs of society. Feliciano Campelo, the beloved employee of the Mayor's Office of Public Works, an exceptionally well-liked and well-regarded public servant, received the news of his beloved wife's death with implacable courage.

The only implacable thing about Feliciano after the death of his wife was his despair. Despair brought on by the absence of his wife's honey-colored curls and heart-shaped mouth, despair on account of the six children who would now suffer even worse neglect, were Feliciano to raise them on his own.

He appealed to the heavens for help and help arrived, though not from the heavens. It came from a few blocks away in the form of Dalva, Feliciano's sister. At thirty, she'd already passed the marriageable age, and had made herself useful by helping her parents in their general store on Rua do Carmo. Dalva offered to take care of the house and the children. After hearing her proposal, Feliciano only refrained from embracing his sister and crying in her arms because his was an era of few embraces and rare episodes of crying among men.

That's how the six children of Feliciano and Maria Rita began to comb their hair and brush their teeth every day. Dalva had found her true calling, which was being busy eighteen hours a day, and Feliciano returned to a life of routine, with dinners at 6.30 in the afternoon, comprised of food that had been cooked on the stove.

Feliciano confided the details of his wife's death to Dalva, including the two seconds witnessed by Antenor. The woman's heart beat strongly for the boy, and while Dalva loved all the children more than anything else, from that moment on she loved Antenor even more. It was Antenor who was the first to be kissed upon arriving home from school, Antenor who got the best pieces of stewed chicken, Antenor whose clothes were mended before the other children's. It was he whom Dalva watched over most closely at night when she went to the children's room to check that everyone was asleep, and it was he who sat on her lap when she read one of the books with the green covers from the *Stories of Monteiro Lobato*, recently purchased by Feliciano.

Now that he lived in a house with waxed floors and spotless bathrooms, homey aromas and white clothes, Antenor nearly forgot those two seconds on that fateful day. What he never forgot was his mother's lawless life, her wild, impotent rages, her inconsequential fits of delirium and the selfishness of her leaving without thinking about her children on the other side of the bedroom door. As far as Antenor was concerned, there was nothing so useless as poetry.

The life he would lead would be the opposite of Maria Rita's. One day Antenor would marry, and his wife would be as wonderful as Dalva. Home and hearth would be the priority. He would give all of himself to the woman he married and would demand in return a life without a trace of the poetry or dreams that did nothing but drive his mother to madness.

It was at that point that Antenor decided upon a wife who seemed absolutely normal – neither ugly nor beautiful, neither fat nor thin, neither tall nor short. A woman whose main qualities were hidden beneath the straw hat she wore as she strolled through the neighborhood. *This Euridice has a head on top of those shoulders*, Antenor thought to himself, without realizing that not only did Euridice have a head above her shoulders but that the contents of that head were well above the average.

Antenor met Euridice on a perfect day one May. He caught the trolley to visit a cousin who lived in the neighborhood of Santa Teresa, and along the way he began to forget the ruckus and dust back in Lapa. Following a night of heavy rain, there wasn't a cloud in the sky and the air was fresh and chilly as it entered his lungs. It seemed to Antenor that Santa Teresa was one of the few places in the city that was still pure, with few automobiles, few trolleys, and not a single skyscraper. Simple and effective, he thought, and he was still lost in thought when he caught sight of the girl framed by fruit crates on Rua Almirante Alexandrino. His aimless thoughts gave way to another consideration which had been percolating in his mind for some time: *Could this be The Girl?*

He decided he was in need of some pears. He stepped off the trolley, chose some fruit and handed over his money to Euridice, looking at her for longer than was necessary to receive his change. Nothing in that girl prompted second thoughts. She wore her hair up in a bun, an apron over her gray dress, not a spot of make-up, and a gaze reserved strictly for adding up each bill. When Euridice gave nothing in return beyond his change, he began to show interest.

'Is Rua Monte Alegre far from here?'

'Not very.'

'Do you think I could go on foot?'

'Perhaps.'

Euridice had passed the first test. It wasn't as if she was feigning a lack of interest in Antenor. She had no interest in Antenor. But Antenor knew who he was. He was a young man of twenty-three, a graduate of the Colégio Pedro II, possessor of a technical degree in accounting, recently hired by the Bank of Brazil, with no ring on his finger and movie-star looks (this last part according to his Aunt Dalva). He couldn't order a coffee, walk into a store, or buy the news-paper without having his hands and his looks examined by all the young women and mothers within sight. They weren't interested in Antenor, but in the idea of Antenor. They put on their finest clothes and make-up, not so that Antenor might show interest in them, but that he might show interest in the idea of them.

But Antenor had no use for mere ideas. He wanted to go straight to what mattered, which was: *Let's see if this girl is capable of getting up each day at the same time, if she won't wait until the sheets are cold to make up the bed, if she'll have the coffee ready at the exact moment I sit down at the table.* He wanted floors so clean he could eat from them, a basket of fresh fruit from the Wednesday market, and the security that comes with someone breathing heavily next to you in the same bed every single night.

He asked his cousin about the girl framed by fruit crates. He learned that her name was Euridice, that she played the recorder like an angel, but after her sister had run away she had never blown another note. He learned that she had completed high school and was good with numbers, but that she had interrupted her studies to help her parents out at the greengrocer's.

As he watched the sunset, Antenor concluded that there was no spot more peaceful or more beautiful in all of Rio. He said goodbye to his cousin around six o'clock and walked to the store. Euridice was still there, her head bent over a notebook.

'Good evening. My name is Antenor and I'd like us to get to know each other a bit better.'

Their courtship went as smoothly as the married life Antenor hoped would follow. Conversations in Euridice's living room, with the glowing lamp on one side and Dona Ana darning socks on the other. Strolls through the neighborhood, with Senhor Manuel keeping an eye on the clock, waiting for them to return. There were no trips to the movies; Euridice's parents didn't want to take the risk.

The formal marriage proposal was made to Senhor Manuel and Dona Ana. Euridice's mother shed some tears and Senhor Manuel – who would have thought? – shed some of his own. He hugged his daughter, saying, 'You're our only daughter, our only daughter.'

Did Euridice want to marry? Perhaps. She considered marriage something rather endemic, something that men and women caught between the age of eighteen and twenty-five. Like the flu, except not quite so bad. What Euridice truly wanted was to travel the world playing her recorder. She wanted to be an engineer and work with numbers. She wanted to transform her parents' greengrocer's into a general store, the general store into a franchise, the franchise into a conglomerate. But she didn't know she wanted all that.

In the years that followed Guida's disappearance, she knew even less. Euridice had quashed her desires, leaving only the exemplary young woman she was on the surface. The one who never raised her voice or her skirt. The one whose only dreams were the dreams her parents had for her. The one who only said 'Yes, senhora,' and 'No, senhor,' without stopping to ask herself what she was saying yes or no to.

Antenor met Euridice while she was in this catatonic stage. He mistook her restraint for balance, and thought: *That's the perfect woman.* He mistook her inertia for mediocrity, and thought: *Here's a woman to marry.* But soon after the wedding she began entertaining those daydreams that so frightened Antenor, and he found himself reminding her of the rules of matrimony at the top of his lungs, telling Euridice that she needed to just sit still.

In the end, Euridice did sit still. After her adventure as a seamstress, she sat still in her post on the sofa, in front of the bookshelf. And that's where she remained – half-drowsed, half-dull, half-dead. The silence that followed was awful, and after a while Antenor stopped wondering whether he'd married a second Dalva or a second Maria Rita. He only wanted Euridice, his Euridice, back. He found himself trying to make conversation.

'Want to walk to the square after dinner?'

'It looks as if the jasmine trees are going to flower next week.'

'It's been a while since you made me those turkey-breast medallions, with the brown stuff on top.'

Euridice responded with weak smiles and *um-hums*. She would agree to everything, as long as she didn't need to say anything else. The woman had decided to take a break of sorts, after the recorder fever, the flirting drama, her kitchen dreams and sewing plans. 'Mama, make me a dress, Mama, make me some oatmeal,' the children would ask, to see if they could cheer her up, and they did – a bit. It was the bigger side of Euridice that they couldn't get through to.

When the doorbell rang, it was Maria who would answer; when the visit was over, it was Maria who shut the door. She even took care of things without even speaking to Euridice. 'Ah, the knives are back from sharpening, let me grab the money for you, senhor.' 'Ah, yes, the bread – add these two loaves to the household account, please.' It was only when she wasn't sure how to solve a problem that she roused Euridice from her contemplative state.

One Wednesday, the doorbell rang and Maria wasn't sure what to do. She walked back into the living room and stood between the bookshelf and her boss.

'Don'Euridice, there's a young woman at the door who says she's your sister.'

CHAPTER 6

Guida. She was still beautiful, but if she had always looked the part of Euridice's older sister, she now appeared to be her much older sister. She had no make-up on and wore her hair up in a bun, clearly arranged to ensure the least amount of work possible. In one hand she held the suitcase that had disappeared with her from the Rua Almirante Alexandrino. In the other, a chubby little boy, more or less Cecilia's age. She wore a beige coat over a green dress.

'May I come in?'

Of all the hugs Euridice had received in her life, that was the strangest. It was a hug that seemed to say, 'Let me touch you to see if you really exist, if you're really standing here before me.' It was true: that was Guida, but not the same Guida as before, a fact that became clear after hearing her sister's story.

Marcos and Guida had met one Saturday afternoon outside the Cine Odeon. He had been standing in the doorway since the beginning of the show, reasoning that if the girl with the long eyelashes had gone inside, she'd also have to leave. Guida walked out two hours later with a group of friends. She kept on walking even after he tried to introduce himself, and she didn't stop walking, not even after he followed her to Cavé Pastries, where she ordered a chocolate eclair and removed her white gloves to display her long fingers as she ate.

All that walking was Guida's way of turning the boy into a sort of train for her dress. She wanted to stroll around just to watch Marcos following her every step. After all, wasn't that love, according to the magazines, films, and the romantic novels from the *Young Ladies' Library* series? It was the woman's job to startle the man with her beauty, and it was the man's job to fight for this woman after the first few moments of paralysis brought on by the startling beauty of The Chosen One.

Marcos played his role. For three Saturdays in a row, he waited for Guida to leave the cinema. Guida also played her part, ignoring the young man so that the next week he would return with even greater interest. After a month, she agreed to let Marcos sit with her as she ate her eclair. Guida nibbled at the confection with particular fervor, bringing her fingers to her lips when they became covered in chocolate, something that seemed to happen more frequently since her admirer showed up. Marcos's eyes drifted between the eclair and the girl's mouth.

The following week, Guida's parents were informed of the courtship. Marcos paid a visit to the apartment in Santa Teresa, spent the afternoon holding on to his hat and responding to the couple's questions in monosyllables. Senhor Manuel and Dona Ana were suspicious. Marcos was much too refined. Much too polite. Much too careful with his appearance. Those nails of this – were they manicured? *Good Lord.*

Marcos's parents did not look favorably upon their son's courtship either. In fact, in the beginning, they didn't look upon it at all, because the boy, who wasn't stupid, thought it better to delay the first meeting between his new love and his family. What they did notice, however, was that Marcos became much happier from one moment to the next, and they grew suspicious. He was the youngest of six children, and the only one who was still a bachelor. A good catch, whom his parents wished to see marry an equally good catch. That's how it had been with their other children, and that's how it had been with Marcos's parents.

For three centuries, the members of that family had married among themselves. It was the only way to keep the entire set of English porcelain and silverware in the family and to serve, on that porcelain and with that silverware, a series of feasts that would no longer be possible were the children to marry outside of the family. Inside the mansion, Marcos wasn't Marcos, but Marcos Godoy de Moraes. His father, Augusto Moraes, had married Mariana Godoy, both of them descendants of Moraes Godoy and Godoy

Moraeses. Every now and then there would appear a Pádua, or a Castro, but the Moraeses and Godoys had reproduced sufficiently to make matrimonial decisions among cousins minimally exciting, such that variations on the same theme had remained a constant throughout the colonial, imperial, and republican eras.

This continual interfamilial fornication resulted in men and women who all looked rather alike. The men boasted enormous cheeks, and heads that went bald before thirty. The women were born and grew up without waistlines, acquiring a rectangular shape early in childhood. They had an abundance of body hair, and while some waxed their upper lips, others had no problem with allowing their mustaches to grow. And they all resembled one another, principally, in the bank accounts they held, the number of properties they owned, and in their vaults replete with gold coins and pink pearl necklaces.

Every now and then, one of the Godoys or the Moraeses cast off the curse of resemblance. For this they owed thanks to God and to their mothers, who, feeling a fire beneath the frills of their skirts, had arranged for it to be extinguished through the years by two priests, three doctors, an explorer lost among the mountains of Rio, and five young black men. This was the case with Marcos, who was larger and more fair-skinned at birth than he should have been, increasing the family's belief in the evolution of the species, and his mother's belief in the Brazilian theater. It had been in the Municipal Theater that she had met a svelte actor, who was responsible for bringing some excitement to her otherwise staid and middle-aged life.

Marcos's father had grown up on one of the five coffee plantations his family maintained in the Paraiba Valley. After the 1929 crash, he sold four of his properties and moved his family closer to the seat of the federal government. He decorated their stately home with settees and loveseats brought from one of the plantations, made by the master carpenter to Emperor Dom Pedro II. He soon found that it was much easier and more lucrative to make a living from politics alone, instead of mixing politics and coffee production, as his parents and grandparents had done. Before running for the Brazilian senate, he made use of his many contacts to take his first bureaucratic measures as chief of staff to the city's mayor.

Marcos shared the mansion in Botafogo with his parents, his three brothers, and their wives. Two of them had begun their political ascent, becoming hand in glove with the highest rung of the Vargas government, to later become *the* hand and *the* glove of the highest rung of the Vargas government: Francisco Godoy was named director of the National Department of Coffee and Armando Godoy became president of the Federal Council of Public Works, an institution so abstract in its conception that not even he knew its purpose. Paulo Godoy graduated from law school, where he made some friends, who had other friends, who said he ought not to spread the word but soon the government would create the Federal Workers' Court. He soon became the youngest judge in Brazil.

Marcos's sisters didn't live in the mansion in Botafogo. One married a cousin who had an unshakable belief in coffee production and in his title of Baron of Itaimzim, which had been in the family since his great-great-grandfather's time. The Baron and Baroness of Itaimzim would spend the next fifty years sitting in the drawing room of their mansion, watching the plaster fall from the walls. His other sister married a diplomat and was at that moment in a Paris cafe, ordering more champagne and discussing with strangers the meteoric liberation of Latina women.

Perhaps as a result of having been spared the incessant exchange of the same genes, Marcos didn't want to marry a rectangular woman. He looked at his family with a mix of disdain and loathing. They were all peas from the same pod, and what a pod it was. The jokes, the antics, the tendency to stick their bogies beneath the table, the way of scratching their chins while making a face, the sense of superiority and scorn displayed when talking to anyone who wasn't one of them – all of that made Marcos want to be only Marcos, instead of the Marcos with the important last names. Dinners were especially annoying, as his sisters-in-law competed to see who had the best husband, judging their qualities according to the number of jewels each wife wore to dinner.

Marcos felt a constant sense of suffocation. He was uncomfortable not only with what he saw, but with what he didn't see. If he had invested in his talent as a medium, he would have heard spirits revealing their stories of power grabs within the family, about this or that Godoy murdered as a result, about love stories with mustache-less women and men with hair who'd never officially existed, about the many deformed children born throughout the centuries who were eliminated from official family history, literally and figuratively. All those cousins who had left this world for a better one weren't in all that better a place. They still believed they had a right to the family's fortune and remained in a sort of limbo, admiring the earrings of the women of the house and coveting the gold chains across their bosoms, the stress of their presence causing two of Marcos's sisters-in-law to be secretly committed to a reformatory for those suffering from tuberculosis.

The resulting emotional burden weighed the house down to such a degree that the most sensitive among the family swore they gained a few inches in height as soon as they left the mansion. That's how Marcos felt, too. He preferred to spend most of his time at medical school, in the bars of Lapa, and on the streets of the old city center. Unlike his friends, he had no desire to be a twenty-something reveler for all eternity. He didn't want to close down the bars, to try out the latest rendezvous spots, or to attend the samba circles despised by high society but very much in vogue among the bohemian crowd.

The only thing that Marcos wanted was someone to talk to. Someone who would listen to everything that had been left unsaid during his two decades of existence. Someone who could further his sentimental education, interrupted so abruptly when he left the arms of his dearest nursemaid for the chairs of São Bento School, where he learned that to be a man with a capital M he could no longer cry for his nursemaid (*No more hugs! No more kisses!*) or feel sympathy for the cats that had their tails lopped off by the boys who one day would run the country.

On the day he met Guida, Marcos was out looking for this person he could talk to. When he saw the young girl with wavy hair, a knee-length skirt, and a felt hat, he understood that his search was over. He needed only to wait for her to walk back out of the cinema.

Guida did walk back out of the cinema, and the pursuit through the streets of the city center lasted four Saturdays. When they finally spoke, she learned in ten minutes everything that she needed to know: his name was Marcos, he was twenty-one years old, he studied medicine, and had a handsome smile.

Marcos didn't bother explaining his list of important last names, and he was happy that Guida wasn't worried about it. All she wanted was a good provider who had Gary Cooper's looks. A degree in medicine was a guarantee of a middle-class life, the highest of Guida's aspirations. And if Marcos turned his head a bit, his nose looked just like Gary Cooper's.

As time passed, it was inevitable that Marcos would have to reveal the anomalies of his past. 'Yes, sweetheart, I've been to Portugal a couple of times, on the way to Paris. During July vacations, I would go to the plantation in Valença. It was closer than the one in Resende. My father works in politics. But this is a very complicated matter for a girl as pretty as you are.'

Guida soon came to understand that Marcos wasn't born with a silver spoon in his mouth but a golden one. She grew happy when she thought about their children who would have golden spoons, and worried when she considered the idea that his family wouldn't like her. Later she began to think that Marcos only wanted to fool around with her before marrying someone with more of a right to this golden spoon. She decided to cut back on her contact with the boy. His hands were only permitted to touch her hands. Their lips could graze, but only once per week, and nothing behind those lips was allowed to leave other than words. The rest of her body was to be admired from afar, and Guida knew how to draw admiration. She framed her teeth between her half-open lips, showing off the gap in the middle, stretched her thighs as she crossed her legs, and tucked in her belly as she walked with perfect posture.

The couple went out regularly, with Guida orchestrating their every move. 'Today we'll see this film, and then we'll walk to the Colombo for dessert.' Or they'd stay at home, with her steering the conversation. 'Look at this girl's braids,' she would say, flicking through a magazine. 'Do you think my hair would look good like this?'

Yes. Marcos's answer to everything was yes. And then, after three months of trips to the cinema and conversations in the living room (at this point Dona Ana had to take up needlepoint since there were no more socks to darn), Guida thought it was time to expand the limits of their relationship, and that this expansion ought to be made in the direction of Botafogo. She posed the question that Marcos most feared.

'When am I going to meet your parents?'

'Look, look here, sweetheart,' Marcos said. 'Look here. It's just that my father is traveling.'

'But why is he traveling if he works in the mayor's office, and if his boss is the mayor of Rio de Janeiro?'

'It's because he has business in the countryside to take care of. Things you wouldn't understand, my love. This is a very complex subject for a girl as pretty as you are.'

The following Saturday, Guida asked if Marcos's father had finished his 'business in the countryside.'

'Not yet, sweetheart. Perhaps next week.'

The following Saturday, Guida asked again.

Looking at his girlfriend with her crossed arms and pouty lips, Marcos thought the time had come to resolve the 'business in the countryside.' But he still wasn't ready to introduce Guida to his family.

'My poor mother. She suffers from angina.'

Dona Mariana's angina lasted another four weeks. Fearing he'd never again see his girlfriend without her arms crossed, or worse yet, fearing he'd never again see his girlfriend's arms at all, Marcos relented.

'Next Saturday we'll have lunch with my family.'

———

Guida cut her story short when Maria arrived in the living room with a pot of coffee and a tray of biscuits. She accepted a cup and sat back against the sofa.

'Do you remember the week I went to Marcos's house for the first time?'

Euridice took a sip of her coffee, considering her reply.

'It was shortly after our fight, wasn't it? she asked. I'm not sure. You weren't speaking to me then, Guida.'

'I know. We stopped talking. But it was difficult for me, Euridice. I was so involved with Marcos, so worried about him not introducing me to his parents, and... Francisco?'

Guida turned around to see the boy at her side entertaining himself with a comic strip.

'Why don't you go play outside?'

'I don't wanna.'

'It will be good for you, Francisco. Go play outside.'

'I don't wanna.'

'Go play outside, Francisco,' Guida ordered.

'No.'

'Go.'

'No.'

Guida began to wring her hands. Euridice stepped in.

'Perhaps you want to watch some television?'

The boy nodded his head. Euridice turned the television on and little Chico sat cross-legged on the floor. Guida felt a certain relief, but continued to wring her hands.

'I never told you about this lunch. Oh, Euridice, it was during this lunch that my life began to unravel.'

———

That Saturday, Guida had arrived at Marcos's house wearing a new dress with a floral brooch on the lapel, a blue felt hat and a purse across her shoulder. Hoop earrings that looked like gold, and a real gold necklace with an image of Our Lady. First she showed up at the gate, and after introducing herself to the doorman was permitted to walk up to the front door. There, she had to speak to the butler, and was directed to a small room on the right. There she spoke with a serving-maid, and after declining a coffee she could at last sit quietly and wait for Marcos to appear.

She heard the sound of far-off footsteps.

'Hello, sweetheart.'

Marcos kissed Guida on the cheek and took her to the Blue Room, where his family sat together waiting for lunch to be served in the Yellow Room.

Guida learned many things that afternoon. She learned that a gold necklace with the image of Our Lady could be transformed into brass, if seen by the sinister eyes of three elegant young ladies. She learned that it was possible to speak to someone for half an hour without this person absorbing anything that was said, as was the case when she spoke to Marcos's mother. Marcos's mother only knew how to talk about herself; she couldn't stop repeating that she had been The Most Sought After Woman in All the Soirées in Rio, at a time when Rio still had soirées, or that Rua Dona Mariana had been named in honor of her grandmother, Mariana Godoy Moraes, or that she had been a patron of the Brazilian theater for many years, but had recently become more interested in sponsoring these young boys of the national swim team. Guida also learned that Marcos's father did not absorb what she said, but in this case it was because nothing she said was of any importance to him. This became clear to her as she stared at the strange man with his narrow eyes. She learned that eating a steak dinner could drag on for a long time, and that even a dessert as refined as profiteroles could lose its flavor. She learned a great deal about Marcos, who also seemed to be a stranger among those people, and about Marcos's brothers, whose eyes bored into the medallion of Our Lady, and not because they were pious but because the medallion was in the only place they wished to rest their eyes.

When Guida was led from the Yellow Room to the Blue Room, from the Blue Room to the entry room, from the entry room to the hall, from the hall to the front door, and from the front door to the front entrance, she knew that she would never again step through the immense metal gate that closed behind her, and she felt relief.

Marcos accompanied her. They walked to the trolley stop hand-in-hand and without saying a word. The further away from the mansion they got, the greater the anger Guida felt in her chest. Anger at having been treated like a fatty cut of meat by those human aberrations. Marcos's family embodied the cliché of those people who ask, 'Do you know who you're talking to?' But it was they who didn't know who they were talking to. She was Guida Gusmao, the woman who never lowered her head to anyone. Guida Gusmao, who had never known failure, who redoubled her strength when she encountered obstacles. Shortly before they reached the trolley, she squeezed her boyfriend's hand.

'Marcos, I'm going to take you away from this place.'

Two months later they were married, signing the papers in front of a justice of the peace. Guida wore a simple linen dress and held a bouquet of orange blossoms. After the ceremony, they returned to the small house they had rented in Vila Isabel, and only then was Marcos permitted to sleep in the same room as Guida.

Since Marcos's family would never allow them to marry, and Guida's family would never accept a groom without his parents' permission – Guida thought they should marry on their own and live far from both Santa Teresa and Botafogo. Marcos had some savings and would be able to cover the rent until he graduated from medical school, which was only a matter of months away. Diploma in hand, he would open his own practice. As soon as they were settled – with a house, his practice, the sick coming for treatment and providing enough money to pay the bills – Guida would return home and explain that they'd married in secret. Marcos and Guida's family would then expand to include Dona Ana, Senhor Manuel, and Euridice.

'I never wanted to spend so much time without seeing all of you.'

Euridice stared at her sister, fascination in her eyes. It had been a long time since she'd been so interested in something, or in someone.

'But Guida, you never returned.'

Guida cast her eyes to the floor and then began to clean the biscuit crumbs from the center table.

'You know that game "Pin the Tail on the Donkey"?'

'What?'

'The game, "Pin the Tail on the Donkey." When we blindfold the children and tell them to pin the tail on the donkey. That game we played at church parties.'

'Yes…'

'Life is like that game, Euridice. There are times we think we're doing everything just right, but then we realize that we're blindfolded and we can't manage to do anything right at all.'

CHAPTER 7

Guida had never been so happy. She had married the man she loved. She lived in a house that was neither large nor small, but just perfect. She spent the day reading ladies' magazines and the afternoons making herself pretty for her husband. No one knocked on the bathroom door if she lingered, or argued with her when she only wanted to be quiet, or ordered her to tend the cash register at the greengrocer's for a few hours. Sometimes she would invite her neighbors in for coffee and they would trade cake recipes, cleaning tips or beauty secrets. She missed her family, but convinced herself that she would see them soon. It was only a matter of time before Marcos established his practice and she would return victorious to Santa Teresa, a gold wedding ring on her finger and a doctor for a husband.

Marcos, too, had become another man. Or rather, he had been another man before. Now he could be himself.

He was no longer obliged to listen to his mother extol the virtues of his cousins Emengarda or Maria Ester, whom he had found rather plain during vacations spent on the plantation, but whom his mother insisted he reconsider, since young women are like caterpillars – it is impossible to predict the beautiful feminine specimens they will become.

He no longer had to put up with his father pressuring him about his studies, after learning – from trustworthy sources – about Marcos's questionable academic performance, only to be reassured that everything would work out in the end 'because the director of the medical school was a friend of many years.' He no longer had to avoid his sisters-in-law, so well versed in the art of sneaking obscene looks his way. He no longer had to avoid his brothers, who even as adults tried to torture him as they'd done when they were younger, locking him in the chest in their parents' bedroom, at times together with a cockroach. Free of all those familial pressures, Marcos finally managed to relax. It was as though he'd just learned how to breathe.

Towards the end of November, he graduated from the National Academy of Medicine and rented a space for his practice in one of the newly constructed buildings on the Avenida Presidente Vargas. He had a door sign made that read *Marcos Godoy, General Practitioner*. He ordered five white lab coats with the initials M. G. stitched across the right breast pocket. He treated patients from Monday to Thursday, nine to five. Fridays were reserved for Guida, as well as evenings and sometimes dawn.

A few months later, Marcos's happiness was no longer everlasting but rather relative. His practice, which was once so busy that there weren't enough chairs in the waiting room, now saw only one or two patients per day. This was on a good day. On a bad day, it was just Marcos, all alone. The young doctor spent afternoons playing tic-tac-toe in a notebook, trying to defeat himself.

The truth was that Marcos was better equipped to be a natural healer than a general practitioner. Despite having rejected his family, the young man retained the haughtiness of his caste. He thought he could do with his studies what his ancestors had done with Brazil: He thought that money could buy his diploma and that his arrogance would bring him knowledge. His grandfathers and great-grandfathers had been made barons and landowners for much less. Graduating with a medical degree would be the fulfillment of a dream, and with the Monteiro Godoys, dreams were transformed into reality with a snap of the fingers, followed by vast sums of money with which to buy possessions and buy off people, along with a few swords, rifles, and whips to accelerate the process.

Marcos had been right: money had bought his degree. He paid a half-black, half-poor classmate to sign the roll call in his anatomy course. It was this same classmate who took Marcos's exams, in a sophisticated exchange of papers that took place in the back of the exam room at Praia Vermelha.

It was foolproof. The young half-black man had a great deal of talent. So much talent that after graduation he opened a practice and worked in the best hospitals in Rio, leaving behind a life of being half-black for a life of being half-white. Marcos attended a few theory classes, though he performed his homework in a rush. It was in a rush that he opened his notebook, using the brief time he spent sitting on the trolley for matters pertaining to school and the rest for matters pertaining to Guida.

Marcos received his diploma, but there would be no snapping of the fingers capable of bringing him knowledge. When more difficult cases appeared at his practice, he had no idea what to do. A young girl showed up with a stomach ache and went home with a prescription for penicillin. Another showed up with varicose veins and was prescribed penicillin. Scarlet fever? Penicillin. Mumps? Penicillin. Thrombosis? Penicillin. Penicillin and paregoric, the purpose of which Marcos didn't quite understand, but he knew it could do no harm.

Prescribing penicillin wasn't such a grave mistake, since the antibiotic cured half of the illnesses known at that time. The problem was the other half. Illnesses which penicillin couldn't do much about. In these cases, it was up to the patients to cure themselves with either prayers or antibodies. The old lady with thrombosis prayed day after day but lost a leg. The young lady with a stomach ache had plenty of antibodies but soon had an ulcer. Before their lives were touched by misfortune, they paid one last visit to Dr Marcos, who scratched his chin, raised a finger and said, 'Now we just need to adjust the dosage of penicillin.'

The only reason Marcos's practice lasted as long as it did were the physical gifts he'd inherited from the now-forgotten theater actor who'd visited his mother's bedroom. What were the chances that a man like him – tall, refined, with light eyes and a snow-white complexion – could be wreaking havoc with his patients' health?

News of the havoc-wreaking doctor gradually spread across the lips and ears of the housewives of Rio de Janeiro, and Marcos's waiting room was soon empty. By this time, he was driving his pen so intently into his notebook when playing tic-tac-toe that he often tore through the pages. He began to turn off the lights at four in the afternoon, hanging his head as he arrived home and no longer feeling so much joy upon seeing his smiling wife at the front gate.

'There's roast beef for dinner, my love.'

A few weeks later, Marcos announced they would be moving.

'We're going to Piedade, sweetheart. We'll have more peace there, you're going to love it.'

When they moved in the middle of the night, Guida grew suspicious. 'The moving truck could only come at this hour, sweetheart.' The promise of a more peaceful neighborhood only increased her suspicions. Peace, there? Only if Marcos considered the relief one felt after the train passed by their house as some sort of peace.

By that point, married life was no longer so easy. Accustomed to a life amid pergolas and Carrara marble, Marcos had stretched the limits of resilience to rent the house in Vila Isabel. It was small, it was simple, but it had everything he'd needed: Guida in low-cut dresses and lingerie. But after they moved to Piedade, Marcos began to see his surroundings with the eyes of a naturalist writer – even Guida, with her perfumes and soft skin, could no longer filter out reality. The endless drip from the faucet in the only bathroom in the house, the rust on the white marble sink, the corners of the ceilings stained with mold, the floorboards so old they had lifted. Then there were the marks left by old picture frames on the white living-room wall, and the minuscule kitchen with its missing floor tiles.

Worse than the house itself were the surroundings. They lived in front of the train tracks and next to a live poultry market. If they opened the window, they were inundated with dust from the train cars and the smell of chickens; if they closed it, they'd suffocate from the heat. There were so many bloodthirsty mosquitoes that Marcos had to sleep with a pillow covering his face, which made it impossible to admire Guida's curves in the twilight. There were also the neighbor's gamecocks, which began clucking at five in the morning. Their clucking woke the hens in the poultry market, who began clucking even more loudly, and soon there was one big, hellish chorus of clucking chickens that could drive even the most level-headed person to grab a machete and resolve the situation once and for all.

A few months later, Marcos announced he would be moving his practice.

'There's an office in a new building in the Bandeira Square. It's all first-class; there will be no shortage of patients for me there.'

Guida gave her silent approval and served the chickpea soup they were eating nearly every night, adding two slices of sausage for Marcos and one for her. The money her husband left each day for the groceries was slowly coming to an end. Guida's luck was that she grew up in a house of Portuguese immigrants who taught her how to make a decent dinner out of tripe, and a bountiful lunch out of leftovers. But something wasn't right. How was it that she, wife to a doctor, had to pinch pennies to do the weekly groceries when the lady at the end of the block, wife to a Candomblé priest, ate steak five days a week?

The good days at the new practice were also numbered. Soon, Marcos didn't have a single patient to treat. He would slump into the seat on the train ride home, trying to make sense of this strange reality where one could not simply buy one's way to the top. And even if it were possible, he no longer had the money to do so.

That April, Marcos had an epiphany. The March rains that had accumulated in the vases around the house increased the breeding grounds of mosquitoes. The aggressive swarms of insects showed no respect for the mosquito coils set around the house. They were constantly buzzing in Marcos's ears, and he slapped and shook every which way, trying to dodge the little pests. One night Marcos was sure a mosquito had flown into his ear – the *zoom-zoom-zoom* seemed to come from within his own head. He spent hours boxing his own ears.

At 3 a.m., he got up, unsure whether he had slept or not. He had the feeling he'd woken up from a bad dream but was still sleeping, because everything around him was like a nightmare. Marcos was slow, but at that moment he found himself able to make sense of many things. The house so old it looked abandoned, the unbearable dinners of chickpea soup, the roosters, chickens and insects that interrupted life at every turn, the noisy train on its route downtown even before sunrise, the inconvenient lawyer who sought him out alleging it was his fault that a client had lost a leg (*What was that man thinking, that he had some way to create a new leg?*), and, more recently, Guida with her hands on her hips, distrusting of everything, complaining all the time, repeating the same question over and over: 'Why do we have to live such a frugal life?'

Seeing Guida there in the bed wasn't enough to free Marcos from his nightmare. Money certainly did buy happiness. Happiness was a bedroom without mosquitoes, even if this bedroom was found in the macabre mansion in Botafogo. Marcos got up, put on the clothes that hung over the chair and left, leaving a message for his wife on the little table next to the door.

The message was his wedding ring.

'And that's what Marcos did to me, Euridice. He abandoned me then and there, left me to my own devices.'

Ooh, that story was better than a radio soap opera, Maria thought to herself. She had heard everything from behind the kitchen door.

Guida knew that Marcos was leaving when he got up that night. She was awake, and lay there quietly, eyes half-open. There was no sense in holding Marcos back. She'd lost him months ago; the end had begun with the constant material decline in their married life. *Let it be,* she thought. *Everything that goes away one day comes back. I give him less than two weeks before he's back here on his knees, swearing to God and to me that all this will never happen again, begging to be taken back into this house full of pests but without any of those ghosts from that old world in Botafogo.*

When two weeks had passed and Marcos hadn't come back, Guida began to think she didn't know as much as she thought she did. What she did know, however, was that she was pregnant. The young woman spent days feeling nauseous, feeding herself corncakes with malagueta peppers and thinking that she needed to tell Marcos that he was going to be a father. As soon as she felt a bit better, she went to look for him at his practice.

She left the house in high heels and a bordered dress.

A flower on her lapel and red lipstick to draw attention to her mouth when she said *Come back home with us, Marcos*. She walked into the building in the Bandeira Square and asked for Dr Marcos Godoy.

'He no longer works here,' the doorman replied.

'That can't be, senhor. He's a tall man, with a white lab coat. A doctor. Light eyes.'

'The very same, senhora. Every now and then people come looking for him. The other day it was a lawyer, and then a woman who was absolutely outraged, with a daughter wearing an eye-patch.'

Guida felt her heart race. She jumped on the trolley to Botafogo, only to be told at the mansion gate that Marcos had not turned up there. She went to the city hall and asked after Marcos at the mayor's office. She waited two hours, only to receive the news from a secretary that Senhor Godoy had no idea as to his son's whereabouts.

It was already getting dark when she took the trolley back to Piedade. She counted the money they had put away inside a flour jar for emergencies and calculated that it would be enough for two months. She looked around at the items inside the house, considering what she could sell. Marcos's wedding ring would be the first to be pawned. He had also left some very nice shoes and pants, which must be worth something. Finishing her calculations, she was overcome with an urge to wax the floor and clean the bathroom. She passed wood oil over the furniture and used a broom to sweep the cobwebs from the living-room corners. She shook out the rug and wiped the windows with some old newspaper. She changed the bedspread, washed the sheets, and hung them out to dry. She soaked the dishrags and brushed the aluminum pans. She chopped onions for the rice, fried two eggs in olive oil, and sat down to eat her first meal in days.

After tidying up the kitchen, Guida sat down and rubbed the medallion of Our Lady that hung across her chest. Who said she couldn't have the child on her own? She could delay paying rent and flee in the middle of the night, moving to some place where she couldn't be found. She would maintain appearances with the ring on her finger, telling the neighbors she was a widow in search of a job. She needed to find work before her belly became noticeable. By the time her employer discovered her pregnancy it would already be too late, he wouldn't have the courage to send her away. After giving birth, she would find someone to help with the child and would go back to her job.

It will work out, she thought to herself. She could make it happen. She switched off the lamp and stood up to go to bed, perhaps too quickly. She felt her head spin and fell back on to the sofa.

No, that would never work out. What a harebrained idea. How am I going to pass myself off as a widow? Who would give me a job? And even if I managed to find one, who would keep me around after I gave birth? I could say Look, Mr. Bossman, I need to stay at home for a while, maybe three months, who knows, and you'll continue to pay my salary and wait for me to return. And who would the baby stay with? As though there were such a place in the world where women could leave their children in the morning and pick them up after work!

None of it made sense. What made sense was to go back to her parents. Swallow her pride, tell them what had happened, and ask to be accepted back into their home.

The next day, Guida did herself up to go out, this time without high heels or red lipstick. She caught the train, a bus, and the trolley that climbed up to Santa Teresa. The closer she got to home, the greater her desire to no longer be a mother but a daughter once again. She wanted to fit on Dona Ana's lap, to feel her mother's fingers running through her hair, and to sleep like a child who knows that the next day will be every bit as good as the one that has just come to an end. She wanted to be woken up again by her father tickling her, she wanted to eat warm porridge with Euridice, every morning of the week.

She hadn't yet stepped off the trolley when she caught sight of the greengrocer's, and Senhor Manuel's eyes. Her mother and her sister must have been at home making lunch. Father and daughter turned to face each other as she drew closer. Senhor Manuel lowered his gaze when Guida entered the store.

'Papa?'

…

'Papa?'

…

'It's me, Papa. Your daughter, Guida.'

Senhor Manuel didn't look up, and only parted his clenched teeth to put an end to the situation.

'I only have one daughter. Her name is Euridice.'

Guida moved to Estácio in the middle of the night. She was wearing black as she opened the window of her new kitchenette early that morning. She introduced herself to the neighbor as Guida Gusmao, a widow without relatives who had come from the countryside. She told the neighbor across the street that she was looking for work.

After lunch, she left the house to get to know the area. There was a general store and a bakery. Two bars and a few stores selling bric-a-brac. *I could work in one of those*, she thought. In the afternoon, she was overcome with fatigue. She returned home and crept between the sheets.

The move, the search for a job while two months pregnant, the whole thing still seemed a harebrained idea. What she really needed to do was to get rid of her child. Yes, that was it. Guida went to the kitchen, boiled some cinnamon sticks, and poured the liquid into a coffee cup. She only need drink that tea and she would miscarry. Then she would have a new life, and even if this new life wasn't so amazing, Guida knew that one day it would be better.

The tea was scalding, so Guida waited for it to cool. When it had cooled a bit, she still thought it was too hot. Better to wait a little more. Then the tea became cold, too cold.

She held the cup with both hands, her gaze fixed upon the liquid. She was overcome again with fatigue and the need to sleep. *I'll worry about this tomorrow.*

The next day Guida inquired whether help was needed at the general store.

'Do you have any experience?'

'My departed husband had a greengrocer's, which we sold off to pay debts.'

'You know how to operate a cash register?'

'Yes, senhor.'

Senhor José told her the pay and Guida said that sounded just fine. It was good for business to have a pretty young woman at the cash register, and it was good for Guida to be able to pay her bills.

In the months that followed, the pretty young woman began gaining weight, and Senhor José pretended not to notice, until the day Guida called her boss into a corner to tell him in between tears how her husband had left her in that condition before passing away. Her tears softened the heart of Senhor José, who replied, 'That's all right, my child, keep doing your work and later we'll see what we can do.'

Guida knew what to do. She would put the child up for adoption. This was no harebrained idea; it was the only way to carry on with her life. Her belly continued to grow and Guida didn't so much as glance at it. Her bump began to move and Guida pretended it had nothing to do with her. When a tiny foot kicked her in the ribs, she warned the little culprit: 'It's from here to the hospital and from the hospital to the orphanage.'

The first part of the plan worked well. One Sunday morning Guida felt the beginning of her labor pains, and since they were still bearable, she decided to walk to the hospital. She arrived at the square across from the hospital unable to keep her legs together. She couldn't remember what happened next, but she had the impression that she spent two hours (or four, or six) sitting alone at the end of a hallway (or was it a waiting room?). Her body coiled when the pain grew unbearable, until she felt a pain that went far beyond unbearable. She looked down to see her son's head. Nurses appeared and she was taken to the delivery room. She remembered screaming some more and following the orders of people who didn't even know her name. The cry of a child, the filthy floor, blood that seemed to flow from white clothes, people coming and going as though they were out in the bustling streets. Someone put her on a stretcher (or was it a wheelchair?) and she reappeared in a hospital room. When she finally thought that she would be able to rest on the bedsheets full of hairs and fresh stains from other women, they delivered her a little white package.

'I don't want this baby here.'

'We have a shortage of cribs at the hospital.'

The old Guida would have thought it was a curse to sleep alongside the cancer that had just been extracted from her belly. But at that moment, Guida was capable of opting for death if breathing meant she would have to make any extra effort. She found a comfortable position next to the child and began to fall asleep, but as soon as she closed her eyes she opened them again in desperation. *The little package is going to fall!* She turned around to embrace her baby. If earlier she had wanted to lose her son, now she felt willing to lose everything but her son.

Guida nestled the baby against her breast and felt peace.

It's so good to have you here, Francisco.

Never again would she be alone.

CHAPTER 8

When Guida returned home she found a bag full of tiny clothes and cloth diapers at the door. A crib appeared from nowhere, along with a pacifier, some baby bottles, and a little rattle. At that time, any child of a single mother in Estácio gained the whole neighborhood as godparents. Guida hadn't been the first to appear alone with some madcap story. There were many young girls deflowered and lost, many who changed marital status overnight following some lapse.

Everyone who could help did, and in a case such as Guida's, everyone could, and did, help. The neighbor across the street sent a pan of porridge ('It helps with milk production'). The next-door neighbor offered to do the laundry ('You still don't have your strength back'). Yet another neighbor brought a crocheted blanket and little red shoes ('For good luck'). She asked if Guida knew Filomena.

'Filomena?'

Filomena had been the most sought-after prostitute in Estácio. She wasn't the most beautiful or the most experienced, but she had such a beautiful smile that the men liked to lay their heads on her breast afterward. Until the smile disappeared, along with her teeth full of cavities. The syphilis appeared next, leaving her face covered in rashes. She lost all her clients, and only avoided starving to death because the neighborhood rallied round her, repaying the food and shelter she had provided over the years to those who had nowhere to turn. As far as Filomena was concerned, money was like air – sometimes it came in, sometimes it went out.

Filomena had no plans to live off favors, so she began to take care of a child here and there while their mothers worked. Both mother and child were so pleased that other mothers soon took note, and then others still. Filomena became the most sought-after babysitter in Estácio. Her three-bedroom house took in children night and day.

'I don't care for more than seven at a time,' she said when mother number eight appeared at her door. 'Try Maria da Penha. Or Efigenia.'

The mother smacked her lips and asked when Filomena would have an opening.

'When these I have now reach school age, I'll let you know. Put your name down in this notebook.'

The mother wrote her name, beneath a list of others.

Filomena had unique methods of discipline, which didn't involve spankings. She had the voice of a siren, capable of making anyone obey. At naptime, the children only wanted to sleep at her side. Filomena cuddled one on her right, the other on her left, set a third on her chest, arranged a few others around her and they slept together in the bed, the woman caught in a web of children. She walked through the house with a train of kids, since none of them wanted to be far from her.

The prostitutes and the factory workers didn't mind leaving their kids in the care of such a ravaged woman. The children would beg to see their babysitter and throw a fit when it was time to go home.

'Don't cry, Paulinho, you'll be back tomorrow,' Filomena would say, prying herself free from a little blond boy.

No one had ever seen Filomena sad or grumpy. She was always smiling or laughing. She covered her lips so as not to scare others, but if something really made her laugh she would forget, and her chuckles revealed tonsils and rotting cavities.

Filomena couldn't refuse a single mother, especially one as weak as Guida. 'Give you just a poke and you'd fall right over,' she said when they first met. The woman also had a weakness for newborns. When she took one up against her breast she remembered the eight children she'd had. Five had been sent for adoption and three had been suffocated by her companion of circumstance in the back of the tenement building.

'They're my little angels waiting for me in heaven,' she would say, with a toothless smile and awful bad breath.

Filomena invited Guida to spend some time in her home until she recovered from her pregnancy. Guida accepted, not only because she was alone, but because that woman brought her a peace she hadn't felt for ages. It was a peace like the one she'd felt when she was still single, when she would nap in the living room to the sound of Euridice's recorder. A peace that she didn't know how to identify until much later, when she no longer had any.

It was there, in a bedroom in Filomena's house, next to a tiny white crib with iron bars, to the sound of children playing in the living room, that Guida finally managed to rest.

Filomena taught Guida to place a piece of damp cotton on her son's head 'to cure the hiccups.' She told the young mother to avoid beans, 'so that the boy doesn't get colic.' She ordered Guida to spend three months cramped inside a compression garment, 'because you may be recovering but you're not dead, and the men think they are holding a post if they embrace a woman without a waist.' The baby had to eat fish mush twice a week, 'to grow up an intelligent boy.' It was Filomena herself who chose the fish heads for Chico's mush. She would arrive at the farmer's market for the pre-closing sell-off, and the vendors set aside the best of the worst parts of the fish that were headed for the trash.

'I thought you weren't going to show today, Filomena.'

'How could I not, Senhor Joel? My little Chico needs his fish. See what I can take for fifteen *réis*.'

Filomena would return home with a smelly package, smiling at everyone she met along the way.

The months passed. Guida was up and running around, Chico was able to walk supporting himself against the wall, but there were no plans to leave Filomena's house. Guida began to help with the children, because whoever can care for one can care for two, three, or four. Filomena accepted this permanent guest, because whoever can feed one mouth can feed two, three, four, or ten. Guida canceled her rent, called a man with a hand-pulled cart to take her few belongings to Filomena's house, and hung a painting of Our Lady of Aparecida on the wall above Chico's crib. And so a new family was formed, composed of Chico, his two mothers, and his numerous siblings.

First, Guida recovered from childbirth, and later, from her abandonment. Who said she couldn't raise her child without its father? She was already doing it. The young woman once again stood up straight and proud, holding her head high as she walked the narrow sidewalks of Estácio.

So much self-assurance struck men dumb. When Guida walked by, they couldn't close their jaws. They would take advantage of their already open mouths to venture an invitation to go out, which only ever resulted in Guida turning her head, closing her eyes, and putting an end to the conversation.

She didn't want anything to do with love affairs. The only man in her life was Chico. When the boy woke in the middle of the night he would run to Guida's bed, and it was so good to be together with his mother that he began to wake up every night. After months of nights spent snuggled up to one another, Guida had to assume a firmer stance. 'You're a little man now, you have to sleep in your own bed.' Chico went back to sleeping in his bed, and then it was Guida who would wake up in the middle of the night, feeling the absence of her boy.

If Guida had a better half, it was Filomena, half-sister, half-mother, and half-associate. Guida instituted professional standards to Filomena's business, which up until then had worked on a *pay-when-you-can* basis. As a result, when the time came to settle the bills, all was up to a *God have mercy*. The price for childcare went up and now there was a cut-off time for dropping off the children in the morning. Once a week, mothers were to send clean towels for their children's baths, and whoever showed up after pick-up time paid a tad more.

'You're an angel who appeared in my life,' Filomena would say, her mouth full of the new dentures she had bought with the additional money that was now coming her way.

'You're the angel, Filomena,' Guida would answer.

Guida and Filomena bought a General Electric radio. They gave the sofa new upholstery, since the old one was threadbare. They fixed the water leaks in the bathroom and on the roof. They painted the front of the house and replaced the broken window. Guida decorated her bedroom using wallpaper with stripes and country flowers just like the design she'd seen in the *Young Ladies' Journal*. The new curtains were made of light-blue voile, the same color chosen for the ruffled bedspread. She bought a dressing table and covered the tabletop with perfumes from the department store. In one corner of the room, clashing with the decor, was little Chico's bed, covered with a white piqué bedspread.

During the day, Guida liked to peek her head through the bedroom door to admire her decorating work and consider whether things were good as they were or if a little something more was needed. That's how she acquired three small paintings of tulips and a little desk for Chico to do his homework. She decided that some pink pillows for the headboard of her bed would provide the finishing touch.

'Salmon-colored pillows,' Guida said, standing in the door and repeating an expression she'd just heard on the radio (she herself had never seen a salmon).

The following day she went to the fabric stores on the Rua Buenos Aires. She chose the biggest one of all, walking right past the fabrics lying out on the sales counter. She looked for the shelf with the highest-quality fabrics and called to the salesman.

'Could you please give me three meters of this silk grosgrain in a salmon color, senhor?' she asked the man, whose jaw had already dropped as he looked at the gap between Guida's front teeth.

'You mean this light-pink, senhora?'

'Yes, this salmon-pink.'

She watched Euridice enter the store. A Euridice looking every bit her own woman, but with the same fixed air she'd always had, which she now used to peruse the fabrics on the sales counter. She recognized that gaze. When Euridice set her mind to something, the rest of the world became smoke. Guida could have stood there, right next to her sister, and she too would be nothing more than smoke. Euridice looked at each bit of fabric, took a tiny notebook from her pocket to verify what appeared to be measurements, and asked the salesman to cut her half a dozen lengths of fabric.

Guida leaned up against a pillar, unsure what to do. She could see the chickenpox scar on her sister's temple. She could smell the Leite de Rosas cream that Euridice still applied to her face. She could see the pendant of Our Lady her sister wore across her chest, identical to the one that hung at that moment across her own chest. If she had reached out, she would have been able to touch her. Was it right to wake her sister from her trance? She missed her immensely, but her desire to appear victorious was greater still. Even though it was beautifully decorated, her room was still in Estácio, and her son had no father. Her painted red fingernails were still employed changing the diapers of other people's children, and her survival still depended on a partnership with a former prostitute. She believed that one day all this would change, and that it was not the moment to walk up to her sister. She waited as Euridice paid for the fabrics, followed her to the city center, and sat in the last seat on the trolley her sister took.

'And that's how I found out where you lived,' Guida said.

'How long ago was this?'

'Not so long. It was last year. You were wearing a light-yellow dress with white stripes along the hem.'

'I know which one you're talking about. I made it, that dress.'

'You made that dress? When did you learn to sew?'

'Just last year, actually.' Euridice looked towards the bookshelf in front of her. 'But now I've set that aside.'

While Guida recovered from her abandonment, Chico continued to grow, a happy child in his early years, and not so happy in the years that followed.

When he was still very young, Chico thought that all other families were just like his. All children had two mothers, and their mothers were as sweet as his (but his mothers were the sweetest of all). He believed that if he ate up the ants that crawled around his fish mush he would gain superhero eyes, because 'ants are good for the eyes.' He thought that when he got a bump on his head a little chick would emerge from behind the lump. He thought the kettle whistled because it was alive, and that if he ate too many lollipops his tongue would turn red forever. He believed that Captain America lived in a faraway land behind the nearby mountain.

As he grew up, he began to realize things weren't quite like that. Families like his did not exist. He had to have a father, like the one in his schoolbooks, with a dark suit and slicked-back hair. People only had one mother, and siblings could come in great numbers, but they didn't come and go like his. He started to suspect that ants were only good for the eyes when one or two fell into the porridge and Guida was too tired to pull them out. The bumps did nothing but hurt, though he still secretly hoped that one day he'd see a chick hatch from them. Why the kettle whistled he still didn't know, but it certainly wasn't alive. His tongue would indeed turn bright red forever if he ate too many lollipops, and this, his two mothers swore, was the absolute truth. As for Captain America, he didn't live behind the mountain. He lived in a place that could be reached only by plane. The man who lived behind the mountain was Saci-Pererê, the one-legged devil in the red cap who always went missing with some household item or another.

By the time he reached the age of ten, Chico was sure he knew everything. His two mothers were tarts, because that was the word he'd heard from one of his classmates, who Chico challenged to a fight even though he wasn't sure what a tart was. He arrived home covered in blood and got an earful from Guida, who later regretted her words and made him some porridge. Guida was so worried about her son's swollen face that she herself removed the ants from his bowl. 'This thing about ants, it's a lie, isn't it, Mama?' She changed the subject. By now Chico knew that no chick would come from the bump that formed on his forehead after the fight, and that the kettle whistled because of the steam, as it did that night. Aside from his wounds he also had a chest full of mucus, so Filomena boiled some water with eucalyptus extract. Then she gave him a lollipop and didn't even bother to say that his tongue would turn bright red forever. How good were those nights when he was feeling sick; his mama Guida would let him sleep in her bed so that he wouldn't be afraid of all those monsters who lived behind the mountain, since he already knew that Captain America lived far away and would never arrive in time to save everyone.

In spite of the lollipops, affection and bowls of porridge, Chico grew up a bit resentful that, while his life was very good, it wasn't life as it was supposed to be. That he had two mothers who were as sweet as they were scorned. Why had a woman crossed the street and spit as she muttered *harlot* when she saw Filomena walking by? Why had they called his mama Guida a *lady of the night*, if he had never seen his mama outside the house after 6 p.m.? Why could Filomena only arrive at church after Mass had begun and leave shortly before it ended? Everything was wrong, he thought, and the more he learned about the world the angrier he became.

When he was eleven, Chico turned from a bit resentful to extremely resentful. Filomena, his mama Filomena, began to feel a pain in her breast, caused by an enormous lump. One afternoon she came back from the hospital without a smile on her face, and cancer became a term even more unwelcome than tart, harlot, and lady of the night. Seeing the despondency in Chico's eyes, Filomena began to smile again. 'Don't you worry, it's nothing!' She tried pulling the boy on to her lap but gave a yelp as soon as their bodies touched. The pain in her breast was greater than her ability to disguise it.

Guida and Filomena sent away half of the children who had been coming to the house. Filomena spent days moaning in the bedroom while Guida grew new arms and legs to be able to care for both the children and her friend. Chico asked to help, but was ignored by his mother. 'Your job is to study and get good grades.' The boy sank his head into his books and lost himself in the stories. Whenever he looked up he decided everything around him was awful, so he disappeared back inside his book.

Little by little: that's how Filomena passed away. The radiotherapy served only to leave burns on her arms, the breast surgery served only to make her even weaker. The cancer spread through her organs like mercury through a thermometer; not a single doctor managed to wrench it from her. Filomena and her cancer inhabited the same body, but the cancer only gained space, whereas Filomena lost it. She knew that she was departing, it was only a matter of time. The problem was that time was passing slowly.

'Oh for criminy, I'm still here!' Filomena would say when she woke from a disturbed sleep.

The cancer had spread to her head, her legs, and between her ribs. The doctors could do little but save her some time in the waiting-line and provide words of encouragement in which they did not believe.

Death would not come. The woman was not so much a woman anymore, rather a pile of wounds sprawled across the bed, but death refused to come. During the day she did not speak, at night she only moaned, and the death that would provide release was nowhere to be found. When Chico was at school, she'd repeat, 'I want to die, I want to die!' God heard her words and would respond, 'That's fine, but not today.' Filomena would ask, 'If not today, when, my God?' God would respond, 'When the time is right.'

The right time was a time that never arrived. Whoever saw Filomena on her way to the hospital turned the other way so as not to see her; those who lived nearby covered their ears so as not to hear her. Mothers began to pull their children from her care, and in the end the only people remaining in the house were Guida, Chico with his head stuck in his books, and thirty percent of Filomena.

The savings put away in the flour jar would be enough to sustain them for a few months of eating chickpea soup, but Guida had more important matters to worry about.

'Give me the injection, give me the injection,' Filomena implored between moans.

The daily dose of morphine given to her at the hospital couldn't keep up with so much cancer. Guida counted the money in the jar and went to the pharmacy.

'Good morning, Senhor Pedro. Could you get me a few vials of morphine?'

'Morphine? That I can't do, Dona Guida. Only with a doctor's authorization.'

'I'll pay well, Senhor Pedro.'

She tried to convince him with a report on the previous night at home.

'It's for Filomena. She got up in the middle of the night and tried to run away from home, said she wasn't going to bring us so much sadness anymore. She passed out in the hallway and we had to carry her back to bed. She woke up delirious, saying that they'd shut the gate to heaven, and that she could see her eight children on the other side. That no matter how much she shouted and shook the rails, no one came to open it.'

'It's an addictive drug, you know, senhora…'

'How much, Senhor Pedro? I'll pay anything.'

The extra dose cost half of their savings. The second cost the other half. The third cost the necklace with the medallion of Our Lady that Guida never removed from around her neck. The fourth dose cost Guida sprawled across the rug in the back of the pharmacy, with Senhor Pedro panting above her. The fifth dose cost the same thing, and the sixth dose wasn't necessary. Filomena left the world in the midst of morphine dreams, the way Guida had wanted it.

Filomena arrived in heaven, still high from the morphine, and finally found the gate was open. With each step she took she felt a bit better. After a few meters, she was as strong as she had been as a fifteen-year-old girl.

'So beautiful,' said an angel standing nearby.

'Me, beautiful?' Filomena asked, and the angel responded, 'Yes, you. Beautiful,' and handed her a mirror. Filomena saw her perfect skin and white teeth. She was so happy that she gave a kiss to the first person she saw in front of her.

'What kind of manners are those, Filomena?'

'Good manners, senhor!' she said, and laughed out loud.

'All right, Filomena,' said Saint Peter. 'Welcome. Your three little angels are over there waiting for you.'

Saint Peter knew that hers were good manners there in heaven. He had also laughed out loud when he'd arrived and seen his own face as good as new. You need to have seen what his teeth were like on earth. Or his syphilis scars.

CHAPTER 9

During the final days of her cancer, Filomena became addicted to morphine, and Senhor Pedro to Guida. Even after Filomena's burial, the pharmacy owner never tired of seeking out the young woman to conclude unfinished business in the back of the pharmacy. Since Guida no longer had any need for morphine injections, and needed a great deal of peace, her responses to Senhor Pedro were variations on 'No' in the beginning and threats to file a complaint in the end.

'If you keep this up, senhor, I'm going straight to the police to speak with the commissioner.'

'Go ahead. The commissioner's going to laugh in your face, that's what's going to happen!' And to reinforce his point, Senhor Pedro laughed in Guida's face right then and there.

Guida turned her back and tried to think about other things. She was Guida Gusmao, the woman who only slept with those she wanted to sleep with, and when she wanted to sleep with them.

After Filomena's death, Chico grew so resentful that Guida allowed him to sleep in her bed once again. A mother's body is an excellent remedy for rage. They held each other beneath the covers, Guida believing she was protecting her son, her son believing he was protecting his mother. Guida breathed deeply so that Chico would think she was sleeping, Chico breathed deeply so that Guida would think he was sleeping. They would fall asleep together. Guida would wake up after a short while and resume taking shallow breaths.

It was no use spreading the news through the neighborhood that she was once again accepting children under her care. The mothers of Estácio had found other babysitters, for better prices than those demanded by Guida. The flour jar where she put away money contained neither money nor flour. The end of the month was arriving, and the landlord had already begun to look at Guida with hungry eyes.

She found work as a cashier at a haberdashery in Rio Comprido. It was a narrow and dark store that received its share of dust from the trolleys and buses going up and down the Rua do Bispo. The store belonged to a Turkish lady with enormous breasts, which appeared even larger in the printed dresses she wore. Dona Amira had been a widow for years, and in order to survive as the owner of her business and her fate she'd discovered she needed to act like a man. Not even the teardrop earrings and long nails managed to give her the slightest feminine air. Everyone in the neighborhood showed respect for her unsmiling *Good mornings*, her pursed lips and her complete lack of interest in anything other than needles, scissors, and thimbles.

The tiny store on the Rua do Bispo was Dona Amira's estate. There, she gave orders and bellowed commands. A few minutes' lateness would be docked from Guida's paycheck. Free time at the cash register was time that could be spent doing other work, so Guida had to make the rounds through the store with the duster. Or the broom, or a damp cloth over the glass showcase, and what did that bird-brained Guida think she was doing with the duster on the other side of the haberdashery? *There's a woman at the cash register trying to buy bobs of thread!* Incompetence was something that irritated Dona Amira to no end, and since she needed motives for irritation in order to feel alive, Guida soon became incompetent. 'You're incompetent!' she would say, and Guida would lower her head.

Guida knew that her incompetence was related to the lack of love in Dona Amira's life, so she didn't think much of it. She knew that her work was related to her son's wellbeing, and so she accepted the situation. Guida also knew that it was better to have a woman as a boss than a man, even if this woman was capable of transforming a haberdashery into purgatory. Better to be in purgatory than in some back room sprawled beneath her boss.

What's more, everything was going to get better the following month, when Guida's 'training period' would come to an end and she would finally earn a full minimum wage and have her work documents signed. Dona Amira had hired Guida on the condition that she undergo a three-month tryout period, earning only half the salary. According to the Turkish woman, ninety days were what was needed to ensure that she could use the cash register. Guida had accepted. Not only because there were no other conditions to be accepted, but because this Dona Amira, so versatile in the art of keeping employees under her thumb, gave Guida an advance, which allowed the young woman to pay the month's rent and made her feel indebted to her boss from the outset.

After spending days receiving orders Guida would return home wiped out, her skin covered in a dusty film. Chico would either be reading a book in the living room or reading a book in the bedroom. Mother and son ate dinner together and in silence. Guida had nothing to say about work, and Chico didn't want to talk about school. They felt the absence of the noise of children and of Filomena's laughter. Eating in silence was like eating with Filomena, the emptiness reminding those left behind of the space she had once occupied.

One July night Chico complained of a sore throat, and Guida prepared a saltwater rinse. He had a bit of fever, so Guida gave him aspirin. A few days later, the boy couldn't get out of bed. He spent the morning in a fetal position beneath the sheets, trying not to moan.

Chico had contracted rheumatic fever. He would need injections of Benzetacil, cortisone, and heart medicine.

'How long will the treatment last, doctor?' Guida asked, wringing her hands.

'Until he turns eighteen.'

Guida continued wringing her hands, as though she might find a few *cruzeiros* hidden in between her fingers. She was never very good at math (although she was good at covering up her errors at the cash register at the haberdashery), but it wasn't necessary to add up the cost of all the medicines the doctor prescribed and multiply that by the twelve months in the year and the seven years of treatment to know that she would never be able to afford it all.

Or perhaps she would.

She went back home to work out a budget. She didn't know much beyond being a cashier. Guida only knew about decoration, about styling hair, make-up, and nail polish... So that was it. Guida could open up a salon at home. She could work on Saturdays and Sundays, and there'd be no lack of clients. All the women in Estácio coveted her looks and appearances, and deep down wanted to look like her.

She requested another advance from Dona Amira, who curled her lips even more but did not refuse. Guida bought brushes, bobby pins, nail polish, nail clippers. She moved the dressing table from the bedroom to the living room, stacked the women's magazines next to the armchair, and spread the news through the neighborhood that her house was now a beauty salon at weekends.

Guida was truly talented with her hands, and had good taste. Women would arrive in a bit of disarray and leave all done up. The money coming in covered Chico's medicine exactly. The elixir for his heart alone cost four hundred *cruzeiros*! The same as ten days' work at the haberdashery.

That day was the last Saturday of Chico's second month of treatment. Guida had just turned off the living-room lights. Her last client had left and now she was resting in the dark, lying on the sofa. Her feet were swollen, her back ached. She grabbed one of the women's magazines, leafed through it without paying attention to its contents. Of all the hands that touched those magazines hers were the only ones with chipped fingernail polish. The following day, women would turn up again at nine in the morning; Guida would barely have time to sweep the room, make some food, and clean the bathroom. Throw out the garbage full of hair and cotton-balls covered in nail polish, tidy up the pile of magazines, give a bit of affection to Chico, and have the feeling that she had only blinked her eyes during her brief hours of sleep. She felt tired but at peace.

She got up to grab Chico's medicine. She opened the bathroom cabinet, where she kept the Benzetacil injections that she had learned to apply to her son and which hurt both of them so much. It was a thick needle that transported the concentrated liquid and left Chico's backside aching for days. At times, the boy could not leave the bed because of the pain. Friends no longer called him to play football in the yard next to the church; just imagine if a ball were to hit his aching bum. She also grabbed the steroid pills and the bottle with the heart medicine.

As she was leaving the bathroom she tripped on the rug and the hypodermic needle stuck into her palm. She gave a yelp and dropped the medicines. The glass bottle with the heart medicine shattered, forming a dark-red puddle on the floor.

For two seconds Guida thought about calling her son to lick up the medicine that would save his life, and hers. There were eight days of work at the salon on the floor. Eight days brushing the hair of other women and painting nails that weren't hers. Eight days lying to her clients: 'You look beautiful with this hairdo,' 'You have such elegant, long fingers.' Eight days in amongst four weeks of work so intense that Guida had stopped being Guida and had become a cog in a wheel whose purpose she couldn't make out – she knew only that it spun, and that as long as these things gave her a small corner in which to live, a bit to eat, and little Chico's health, they could treat her like a cog and she wouldn't mind.

She could have sat on the toilet seat for half an hour or an hour and a half, crying over spilled medicine, if she hadn't had more important things to worry about. Chico had to take his medicine the next day. The doctor had been clear: missing a single dose would leave her son with chronic heart problems.

She returned to the back room of the pharmacy and beneath the body of Senhor Pedro. The months of abstinence had caused him withdrawal symptoms, which revealed themselves in the drool he let fly over Guida. It was as though he were tasting honey for the first time; he made a mess of himself, a mess of Guida, and held down her arms, the pressure of his hands saying, 'The medicine is mine, and for the medicine to become yours you have to become mine, and everything that is mine is beneath my body and firmly in my hands.'

Guida stared blankly to one side. She waited for the man to finish and left the pharmacy with the medication. Half a month's medicine was now safely hers.

Two days later, she knocked on Euridice's door.

This wasn't exactly the story Guida told to Euridice. Sitting with her legs crossed, having captured her sister's attention, Guida regained a bit of her self-esteem. In the version she told her sister, Filomena was a retired schoolteacher ('Only by working in education can you understand children like she did, Euridice!'). Senhor Pedro was a saint who helped Chico with his medications ('I don't know what would have become of me if that man hadn't wanted to please me so much!'). The part about Marcos, Guida told in its entirety – throwing in 'scoundrel,' 'good-for-nothing,' and 'thin-skinned' for good measure, and revealing details that made Euridice's eyes transform into the shape of marbles.

'Soon after we were married, Marcos asked me what a strainer was for. He'd never seen a strainer, Euridice! I told him it was to remove little bits of fat from the milk, and he told me the milk in his house had always come strained from the kitchen. How is it, Euridice, that a man doesn't even know what a strainer is? Marcos had never cut an orange. One time I put a few on the table after lunch and he cut the fruit sideways, there was no way to eat it anymore, the wedges were unsalvageable. And he was only able to sleep with a pillowcase over his eyes. He said he couldn't get used to the morning sun beating down so close to the bed, that his room in Botafogo had velvet curtains that kept out even the midday sun. A sissy, Euridice, a real sissy.'

Euridice felt a bit relieved to hear the stories that Guida told. It was inevitable that she would compare Marcos to Antenor, who she'd always known was a good husband. At least Antenor knew what a strainer was. A strainer was that thing that his Aunt Dalva and his wife Euridice used when they made orange juice, so he wouldn't die clogged up with pulp.

In the part of the story with Dona Amira, Guida invented a bit more. The sweetest boss. When she received Guida's resignation, she had to sit down to contain her dejection, and said, with a hand over her heart: 'You're a daughter to me, you hear, Guida?

'You should have seen how she cried! But I told her that it was time for me to change my life, and dedicate more time to Chico's education.'

It was exactly because she wasn't a daughter to Dona Amira that Guida was at her sister's house. She set the coffee cup down on the table and sat on the edge of the sofa.

'Well, Euridice, it's time for me to be near Mom and Dad again. I thought that we could go together to their house.

Perhaps Dad won't understand my running away, but Mom – I know Mom is going to forgive me.'

Euridice responded with her eyes cast to the floor.

'Mom died last year.'

Guida brought her hand to her chest, seeking out the pendant of Our Lady that she would never again find there.

No one ever knew exactly what was wrong with Dona Ana. It was an illness that grew almost imperceptibly, day by day. Dona Ana became more and more hunched over and weak. She even left bits of salt cod untouched, and this was a woman who would always finish meals with a bit of bread to clean her plate. When she wasn't feeling sad behind the cash register at the greengrocer's Dona Ana was feeling sad cleaning the house, or sad cooking, or sad simply feeling sad, looking to the frame which held Guida's picture.

Every now and then she would go to a different doctor. It's anemia, it's a lack of vitamins, it's a lack of calcium, they all said. In fact, it was a lack of Guida, but that wasn't in their books, so Dona Ana would go home with a prescription for vitamins and promises that she would improve. You need a tonic for your nerves, for your heart or for your muscles, they'd say. A tonic to forget that her daughter had run away, so she grew sicker by the day, leaving bits of salt cod on her plate and casting her eyes towards the picture frame in search of the only antidote that could make her regain her health.

One day she opened her eyes and decided that there was no reason to leave the bed. She turned to one side, turned to the other, and took a few naps. The next day she opened her eyes and decided there was no reason to turn from one side to the other. On the third day, she didn't open her eyes.

Senhor Manuel went a bit mad after the death of Dona Ana. Like the good Portuguese man that he was, he preferred doing this alone and against the bedroom wall, where he beat his head in anguish during the first seven nights without his wife. He wished he had hair to pull, but now there were but a few strands behind his ears, combed over the top of his head to cover his bald spot. The sparse strands of hair were so precious to him that he thought it better to leave them be. He felt the same remorse in his heart as Guida when she learned of her mother's death. Remorse for things that weren't even his fault, like the rough manner that came from his childhood, and the belief that nothing was as important as honor. It was this belief that had caused Senhor Manuel to disown his own daughter. Better to have a daughter far away and a wife dying bit by bit than to take back the prodigal daughter and transform the shame into something tangible.

When Antenor arrived home that afternoon, he stumbled upon a scene from a soap opera. There was this woman he had never seen before, so beautiful – even as she made a face – flailing her arms, as Euridice consoled her and Maria waited on foot with a glass of sugar water on the silver serving tray. Cecilia and Afonso had arrived home from school a short time before and also stood by watching the scene; they couldn't miss a drama like that. There was also this pudgy little boy with a pouty look on his face who hugged the young woman and rocked back and forth with her to the rhythm of despair.

Antenor didn't even grow angry, because for the first time in a long time he noticed the interest in Euridice's eyes. He liked to see his wife so attentive, even if it was as a supporting actress in this dramatic scene, and even if this scene took place in his living room next to the radio with its toothpick legs, which he had hopes of seeing survive the performance intact.

He decided he could kiss his wife's forehead another time and went straight to the bedroom to change his clothes and put on his slippers. When he came back to the living room the woman had calmed down considerably. She continued rocking back and forth, but now she sobbed quietly in the arms of the boy and Euridice.

When Guida was herself again, she was introduced to Antenor. She had rivers of black make-up running from her eyes, and eyes that didn't pay attention to that. 'A pleasure,' Guida said; 'A pleasure,' Antenor said, and uttered not another word. Euridice took her sister and Chico to the guest bedroom, showed them the bathroom and told them dinner would be served in half an hour.

When the six places at Antenor and Euridice's dinner table were occupied that night, everything seemed perfectly natural. It was natural to host these exotic guests, and it became natural to see them walking through the house, first for a few days, and later for a few months. The routine of phrases traded between Euridice and Antenor, the *good mornings* and *goodbyes*, the sitting together for breakfast, the telephone call he made to his wife after lunch, the kiss on her forehead at five-thirty in the afternoon, the dinners, all took on a deep and implicit meaning: *My sister will stay with us as long as she needs. She will leave when she feels ready, which might happen in a month, a year, or who knows how long.*

Antenor consented. It was good to see Euridice happy, smiling and showering Cecilia and Afonso with kisses. It was good to hear his wife's laughter echo throughout their home. He hadn't even realized she could burst into laughter like that, time after time. He also enjoyed having Guida around. Euridice's sister brought the Guida touch to the Gusmao-Campelo house. The crystal vases were suddenly filled with flowers, the tables had bordered tablecloths, and just look at those new pillows on the sofa. Chico was a quiet boy, living in a world composed mainly of his new school. He was the best student at the best institution in Rio, but he didn't seem to care. The only things he cared about were his books, which unnerved Cecilia slightly. How could a boy who wasn't *all that* ignore the girl who had earned the title of Class Queen, chosen nearly unanimously by the three classes of the sixth grade? (The girl who placed second received eight votes that, according to Cecilia, were bought with cheese bread doled out during recess.)

Every now and then Chico would pull his head out of a book to play button football with Afonso, which Cecilia considered yet another affront. As far as she was concerned, the only buttons worth his attention were those on her dresses. Aside from this minor conflict, the addition of Guida and Chico to the family occurred seamlessly. It was as though the guests had been expected for a long time, as if their arrival was all that was left for the Gusmao-Campelo family to be complete.

It was also the only thing left to add to the rumors that circulated about the household. Zélia spent whole days and nights with her arms and legs crossed, her face and body immune to the world, tapping her feet and wondering what in the world could be so funny on the other side of the wall to make Euridice burst out laughing like that.

An inappropriate sort of laughter, Zélia thought to herself. Everything that went against morals and good manners was inappropriate in her mind, and it was certainly not good manners to show just how happy one was. And who was that woman who was so, so... exotic? And that boy so, so... boyish? Zélia soon found out that they were Euridice's sister and her son. It appeared that the woman had lost her husband in a battle against cancer, which Guida made a point of recounting in detail to the curious neighbor. 'We went to Cleveland for his treatment, we rented a Tudor-style house and spent the winter in the snow. We drank hot chocolate like it was water, Nicanor bought me a fur coat, and Chico learned to ice skate. But as you know, miss, when God calls, no one can pretend not to hear, and God called my dear departed Nicanor, a high-ranking diplomat, a faithful servant of our dear Brazil, a tall and handsome man... You know what they say, Dona Zélia: Over there is becoming more interesting than over here.'

Zélia's heart shriveled with rage. It shriveled and it stayed shriveled, because there was no way for her to find the hair in the dish that was Guida's life. But there was a hair some-where, that she knew.

CHAPTER 10

I should have done this long before, Guida thought to herself during those precious months with her sister. They laughed for any old reason and for no reason at all. They walked together to the grocery store, discussed the fate of soap-opera characters, and spent entire afternoons browsing the display windows of Saenz Pena Square. They only stopped laughing whenever Euridice tried to convince Guida to see their father again. At such moments, her sister made a face just like TV actors do when they want to show that life's adversities are incapable of compromising their character.

'I'll never set foot in Santa Teresa again. Never again.'

The two would walk in silence for a little while until they forgot why they were sad and would then resume enjoying each other's company. Euridice and Guida felt younger than Afonso, Cecilia, and Chico, even more so because the three kids were entering those annoying adolescent years.

Following Cecilia, the time arrived for Afonso and Chico to discover their hormones and, in their case, that thing that sometimes grew painful between their legs. The inopportune swelling required immediate alleviation, for which Chico learned to use the bathroom and Afonso learned to use Maria.

'Careful, or your father will find out,' Maria would say as Afonso pulled his pants back up.

'The heck he will. And if he finds out, you'll lose your job.'

Maria listened and Maria grew quiet. Her three children still needed her, and it even looked as if one of them wouldn't be a good-for-nothing like his father because he liked that studying thing. If just one of her sons moved a step up in life she could die in peace, which was one of the few things she desired. She had even taken a look at the cost of a casket; she'd chosen one made of a light-colored wood with golden handles. She had already begun paying the installments for her plot in the cemetery; there was no way she was going in some common grave. Life hadn't smiled upon her, but she would make sure death treated her better. For Maria, another lifted skirt here or there didn't make much difference. What was the problem in alleviating the boy's suffering? The worst had been her first time. At thirteen she didn't know much and tried resisting, returning home with bloodstains that marked more than an end to her virginity.

But we'll leave Maria here and turn back to Guida, who had recovered from more than a decade of hard knocks for believing in the call of the French Revolution. In spite of having her heart crushed by Marcos, in spite of the long months of solitary pregnancy, in spite of the years spent caring for other people's children, in spite of the endless nights listening to Filomena moan, in spite of the dusty times on the haberdashery floor and the days of acetone wafting through her living room, in spite of all the fluids spilled against her wishes between her legs, Guida bounced back like one of those inflatable toys that always pop up again, no matter how many times you hit them. Each time she rebounded with even more strength, more smiles, and with a stronger belief that her fate was that of a victor.

It was this radiant Guida that Antonio, the owner of the stationery store who was eternally in love with Euridice, came to know. But she was also much more than this. Guida was a bit of Euridice, because they both raised their eyebrows when they liked something they heard, and flashed the same smile as they walked out the door. They were different in many other ways, but Antonio needed nothing more. He only needed to find a way to spend more time close to Euridice, or close to everything that had a bit of Euridice.

The first *good mornings* Antonio uttered to Guida came between stutters, along with an awkward scratching of his neck. Guida thought it was all very cute. She felt protected next to her sister, and why shouldn't she accept the good intentions of this mustachioed man with his shirt buttoned up all the way, the man who only called her 'Senhora Guida', and with so much more respect than all the other 'Senhora Guidas' she'd heard up until then?

Assenting to Antonio's courtship was like leaving the house with a portable radio tuned to the best shows on the Radio Nacional. He made poetry with his phrases, and everything he said appeared to come from the mouth of a songwriter. *Someone like you, just like you, I needed to find. / You're a star among the Milky Way, the mother of royalty. / You are everything that is beautiful in all the world's resplendence.*

Guida would stand before her admirer, drinking in his words. For many years she had been deaf to male advances, and it was good to hear them once again.

After some time hearing how she was an 'immaculate camellia,' a 'graceful nymph,' and a 'dazzling muse,' Guida thought it was time to open her 'alabaster breast' and her 'mouth full of nectar' to add to the vocabulary of their courtship phrases like 'a life together,' 'commitment,' and 'plans.' She could see in Antonio's face the rest of her days. The two of them together in the bachelor's apartment, Chico gaining the father figure he'd never had. Guida ironing clothes in front of the television set, crochet towels beneath the ornaments on the bookshelf, a lifetime free from dinners of chickpea soup. It wasn't exactly love that she felt for Antonio. It was affection, which throughout those months of flirting was promoted to love, to justify her dream of ironing clothes in front of the TV and decorating Chico's room in blue. It was about Chico, in fact, that she wanted to talk on that Saturday afternoon, after they'd ordered pastries and gooseberry juice at the Colombo cafe.

'Antonio, I understand that you have great esteem for me. And that it would be a gift to have me as your companion. But, as you know, I have a son. And I won't leave his side, ever.'

Antonio said nothing for a few seconds. He took his handkerchief from his pocket, wiped the sweat from his forehead and began to scratch at a few red spots that had appeared on his neck.

'Guida, I understand that you have great esteem for me. But, as you know, I have a mother. And I won't leave her side, ever.'

And Guida, who had been leaning in towards Antonio, sat back in her chair.

Dona Eulália was mother to four children, of which Antonio was the youngest. Her father had been the owner of one of the first breweries in Brazil, the Cervejaria Tupā. In the early days, he made the beer at home to the sound of his wife's complaining. When she wasn't feeling queasy because she was pregnant she was feeling queasy because she couldn't stand the smell of fermented mold. 'It's all going to work out, woman,' he said, as he filled casks and printed labels for the bottles. Luiz was a visionary, capable of seeing imminent wealth in the hand-pulled carts that distributed his product throughout the city center. 'It's all going to work out,' he repeated, even when his bottles were refused by the cellars along the quay – more interested in wines from

Portugal, or by the bars of Carioca – more interested in German beer.

It was around this time that the city's essence was defined, and the residents of Rio ceased to be Portuguese immigrants, Turks by birth, Brazilian-born, Chinese expats, half-white, half-mulatto or half-Indian, to become true *Cariocas*. And no sooner had they realized that they were now *Cariocas* than they began to feel a hankering for a glass of ice-cold beer.

A glass of Tupã, please, they started telling dive owners at dusk, thus inventing the habit of a cold one at the end of the day, making Luiz the new republic's first millionaire.

The brewery was moved from the family kitchen to new premises in the industrial zone. The family kitchen was also moved, from the dirt road in Santo Cristo to a ranch house in the city's most desirable southern district. A roast chicken no longer had to last three meals, and Luiz acquired a hefty belly, adorned with a pocket watch that he would retrieve less to check the time than to show that it was made of gold. His three daughters soon had a German governess whom he also liked to show off, sending her to the pastry shop for *fohr-uh French row-uls, please*, which she would always take with a *dank you*.

Eulália was born in the tiny house in Santo Cristo but only began to make sense of the world at the ranch house in Laranjeiras. Her earliest memories were of the long corridor that separated the eight bedrooms from the main drawing room, the bulky thighs of the black women who spent the whole day working in the kitchen, and the lawn with its border of immaculate flowers that remained in bloom no matter the time of year.

When she awoke each morning, it wasn't the image of her mother she saw through the curtains of tulle, but that of her nursemaid, who bathed her, dressed her and combed her hair. Hortencia had more important things to do than care for her daughters. She had to learn how to be rich. Life had been simple back in the days of the home brewery, and when the pile of money appeared she wasn't sure how to act. She would go out in her new carriage to the Rua do Ouvidor, observe the elegance of the ladies in the street, and walk into the French stores, where she bought her fill of hats, parasols, and fans. The problem was matching the accessories with the designer dresses, and during those first few years she was guilty of some excesses. She would show up for Mass in bodices embroidered with gold, and with layers of lacework on her skirts. Her hats could have been slices cut from the Amazon, such was the abundance of plumes, flowers and fruits. Hortencia was at once ignored by the other women and the main topic of their whispered conversations.

On Wednesday nights, she would listen to the sounds of a party coming from a nearby house. Heitor Cordeiro opened his doors to the Carioca elite for a weekly soirée, but Hortencia and Luiz were never invited. They of all people, who lived so close! After all, those were the early years of the republic, when the closed castes of the monarchical era had been replaced by bourgeois meritocracy, so why didn't

Heitor Cordeiro, Bebé Silveira, or Raul Régiz, who organized the finest soirées in Rio, recognize Hortencia and Luiz's new money as a merit to be considered and invite them to enjoy a drink and recite verse?

They were a band of snobs. What Hortencia needed was to become as snobbish as they were. She tightened her corset even further and added yet more fauna and flora to her hats. On his wife's orders, Luiz could only leave the house in a dress coat and top hat, a silk vest, and a plastron. Her daughters were perpetually encased in stiff linen, with shiny lace-up boots that hurt their feet.

The ranch house was also transformed. It lost its country-house air and became a castle of Gothic towers and Moorish doors. The garden soon had a fountain, and the fountain soon had a cherub. Hortencia purchased two porcelain lions to guard the entrance to the house and installed statues of Apollo and Jupiter on the veranda. She bought French armchairs upholstered in silk, chairs with backs of fine fabric, tables encrusted with bronze, and books to decorate the library. She bought so many ornaments that she soon needed crystal cabinets to house them all. After acquiring more cabinets she had to buy more ornaments, and if she happened to go overboard with the ornaments she had to buy yet more cabinets, and so on.

After a few years, the ranch had become one of the most exotic places in Rio de Janeiro. There wasn't a single grande dame who wasn't longing to enter the mansion in her lace-up boots. Hortencia needed only to prepare the invitations and open the doors of her soirées to what became known as the Great Tupã Ball.

Guests could smell the jasmine covering the grand salon walls from the corner opposite the house. After passing the porcelain lions, they were greeted by an albino black man dressed as a court jester. The pony circus that had disappeared that morning from the public square was reassembled in the garden. Two clowns, a sword-swallower, and a human cannonball performed nonstop. An artificial pond was built in the salon, where a swan brought from the countryside could be seen swimming in a sea of Tupã beer. Even an Indian appeared, though he was spared from performing. He was considered indolent for not having learned how to juggle in time for the evening.

Cornish hens, partridges and wild pigeons, egg-yolk threads, foie gras and fruit sorbets, hams with cloves, pork loin, and fillets of whiting were served by twenty-five servants in white Louis XV wigs. Luiz's beer was the only beverage served, sending an explicit message that from that night on the guests would have to swallow not only the beverage, but also their hosts.

Despite all her years leading a modest life, Hortencia had what it took to please high society, which was a bit of imagination and plenty of bad taste. The very next day she began to receive invites to poetry recitals and soirées throughout the city. After some studying of her new friends' schedules, it was decided that she would host a soirée on Monday nights.

The great Ernesto Nazareth would appear at the house to compose and practice on the piano. He only looked up from the keys to drink a beer, and then six more for the road. An abashed Olavo Bilac recited poems and sold ten copies of his first collection to Hortencia, which she didn't read, didn't want to read, and used to line the cage that housed her cockatoos. The Italian artist Angelo Agostini sat in one of the corners of the room and drew caricatures of the guests while Hortencia, dressed up as an odalisque, offered her banqueters a hookah recently brought from Morocco, full of apple smoke with cannabis that had come highly recommended by a friend. Machado de Assis himself, the greatest writer in the history of Brazil, appeared once too, even if he had come in slippers and only to complain of the noise.

Eulália grew up believing that abundance was a birthright. It was normal to have piles of clothes, even with her body growing in inverse proportion to the possibility of her ever wearing them all. Normal to have her shoelaces tied by her nursemaid, normal to feed the fox terrier the pieces of chicken breast denied to the servants. The poor existed so she could wear new gloves and not soil her hands distributing alms after Mass. School existed for her to learn French, and to know how to order a *croissant* in a *boulangerie* during the family vacations in Paris. And the soirées in her house existed for her to meet a suitor of her caliber, marry, and give birth to four children, who would be raised by a nursemaid. Eulália had more important things to worry about than bringing up her own children – being rich, for example.

It was good, intense, and everlasting. Until it wasn't.

Now in his sixties, Luiz was having a hard time getting around. Even as the owner of the largest brewery in Rio he had never forgotten his years of hardship, and he remembered them especially when faced with a juicy thick steak. He was happiest when the meat barely fit on his plate, and he wolfed it down with fries straight out of the frying pan. He could no longer see his feet, but displayed his new figure with pride, as it was the antithesis of how he had looked during his frugal years.

It was written in his destiny that steak would be the death of him, but not because of clogged arteries. As he left the brewery one afternoon, he crossed the street and underestimated the time it would take to reach the sidewalk. One trolley was coming from one direction, another from the other. Luiz sucked in his belly, but still ended up squished between the two. His insides spilled out under the pressure, dirtying the legs of some passengers. The man's casket had to remain closed, because his brains had landed on the arms of a passerby.

Hortencia was devastated. Not only because Luiz was the best man she had ever known, but because she was sure her sons-in-law would run the business into the ground in less than a decade. She was wrong. They ran the business into the ground in less than two years.

The mansion was sold to pay off debts. Hortencia moved to a boarding house with a single bed, a chest full of golden dresses, and a box encrusted in mother-of-pearl that contained the money from the sale of the crystal cabinets and the ornaments. Hers was the last room on the top floor and she only left to eat, go to the bathroom or sit in the sun by the clothesline for an hour every afternoon. She became known as the aristocrat with long dresses, who told stories of grand balls, which at times included an albino black man dressed as a court jester and a swan that swam in a pond of beer. On other occasions, it was the albino black man who swam in the beer and the swan that was dressed as the court jester.

No one believed a word that came out of the poor woman's mouth, but they liked her all the same. When Hortencia lost all the money in her box because she didn't know how to trade in the *mil-réis* coins of the new currency introduced in the forties, the other residents pitched in to pay her rent, allowing her to keep her routine of sunbathing and telling wild stories until her death, at the age of 102.

Unfortunately, Eulália didn't have the same natural ability to adjust to poverty as her mother. She had never known what it was to be poor, and she didn't like it. She'd had the rug pulled out from under her, with everything upon it – from her Italian shoes to the jacaranda furniture. Moving from the mansion to a two-bedroom apartment in the suburbs was a blow to her senses. A blow that removed any bit of sweetness that her indolent personality might have possessed. The walls of those cubicles were claustrophobic, and she couldn't see how a family of six could possibly fit there. Within a few short days, they found the answer. They fit because they had to fit. Eulália grew more ill-humored with each day, and made the life of those around her a living hell.

Eulália's husband, who until then had been known as Onofre Francisco Castro Lima, soon became Onofre the Useless. He came from a family that believed wealth was something endemic. Something that was theirs by birthright, and that they had gained by a simple process of osmosis – they simply needed to remain close to those in power to maintain their privilege. When Onofre's great-grandfather, the Marquis of Ouriçal, disembarked from the ship with the Portuguese royal family, he had the right to one of the finest houses in Rio. Onofre's grandfather had the right to a post in the Customs House, to receive a salary without working. Onofre's father had the right to a distinguished family name, which he traded in to marry the daughter of a slave trafficker. Onofre had the right to what was left of the family name, which he then traded in to marry the daughter of a businessman.

After having his investment in a tranquil future shredded between two trolleys, Onofre wasn't sure what to do. The truth was that he had never known what to do, but now the consequences were more serious. He had six mouths to feed, and after spending several long days trying to think of a solution to his problems, he had no alternative but to stop thinking and start doing something. He managed to get a job in a real-estate agency, but the days he worked were as frequent as leap years. The commissions he earned were even rarer than leap years, and the money that did come in couldn't match their expenses. To run from this dreadful monster called reality, Onofre began to drink. First, just a bit of port wine. Later, a cachaça known as Angel's Piss, capable of corroding stomachs and dissolving livers.

Onofre the Useless died of cirrhosis. Eulália the Bitter took her children out of school and sent them to work. At the end of the month she would seize her sons' earnings and, if the mood struck her, she would give them some change to buy a cigarette – *one* cigarette. She discovered she'd given birth to some truly romantic boys, who barely reached eighteen before announcing marriages to girls who would never meet with their mother's approval. Before leaving the house they each wrote their new address in a little notebook, in handwriting not even a seer could decipher.

Each year, she lost a son. By the time Eulália realized it, the only one left was her youngest, Antonio. She clung to the boy like an octopus, making the apartment her kingdom and Antonio her servant. 'You will never leave me, ever,' she decreed.

It was around that time that she began to experience health problems. Heart palpitations, formication, and ailments mysterious even to the doctors who tended to her. If Eulália had a cough, she thought it was tuberculosis; if she had a headache, it could be a tumor. Each illness arrived with a premonition. If she went to sleep thinking about heartburn she would wake up with a burning sensation. If she went to sleep thinking about her circulation she woke up with swollen feet. Chest colds were transformed into pneumonia; a rash could be psoriasis; and her heart, which had never pounded on account of anyone, suddenly experienced a constant murmur.

Eulália's illnesses grew more frequent during her remaining son's early adult years, when he was the right-hand man of the proprietors of Rio's most popular stationery shop. They worsened when the young man left his job to open his own business, attracting visits from perfumed young women who never seemed to have working pens at home. Eulália improved in the following decade, when Antonio began to grow white hairs and confirmed his only interest was stamp collecting.

It was genetics that made Eulália sick. Not anything present in her own DNA, but in the DNA of her son. Antonio was a big man, with a chest like a shield and tufts of black hair that fell into his eyes, which induced in women the desire to comb it. His perfect teeth made young girls blush when they discovered they were capable of dreaming up other uses for their mouths beyond the usual mealtimes. One young woman fainted in the stationery store after seeing Antonio's biceps exploding beneath his shirt as he lifted a box of paper. She came to a few minutes later in an undesirable location: it was Eulália whose lap she was resting against and who patted her cheeks, the smell of her onion breath filling the young woman's nostrils.

CHAPTER 11

Only two women among the 189 who went to Antonio's stationery store in search of something besides blotting paper managed to break through Eulália's curses. The first was Isabelle Bouquier. Isabelle was daughter to the owner of the largest bookstore in Rio, the Frenchman Jean Bouquier. She played piano, spoke four languages, wasn't ugly, and spent summers in Paris. Isabelle could have had any man who walked down the Rua do Ouvidor or the Boulevard Saint Germain. And, to prove that she could have any man, she wanted one who walked neither down the Rua do Ouvidor or on the streets of Paris. She met Antonio one boring Sunday as she went with her family to see the military band play at the bandstand in the park. The young man's head stuck out among the crowd. He liked to eat popcorn one kernel at a time, and watched the band with the interest others displayed when watching an opera at the municipal theater. After the show, the crowd dispersed and Isabelle was able to assess the rest of Antonio. An alpaca suit, ordinary shoes, and an older lady whom he took by the arm.

The first time Isabelle appeared in the stationery store, she had to face the curled lips of Dona Eulália, who during those years only left the cash register once a day to use the bathroom. But when Antonio's mother learned about the girl's family, the curled lips transformed into a smile, to later curl again to say *Bonjour, comment allez-vous? À bientôt, à bientôt!*

Jean Bouquier was a man with many *contos de réis* in his bank account, not only because he knew how to sell but because he knew what not to buy. From his front door to the street, his house was one of the most luxurious on the Rua Conde de Bonfim. From the front door to the back it was one of the most frugal. He examined the stamps on each letter he received, and those without an ink-stamp were unglued from the envelope to be reused for a future missive. His shoes passed through a peculiar metamorphosis, which allowed Jean to wear the same pair he'd had since he'd turned eighteen: he would send the soles to be redone from time to time, and if the sole was in good shape but the shoe worn, he kept the sole to make a new pair. The coffee grains used one day were reused the next, and the few times he ate at restaurants he returned his plate as if it had been licked clean. Jean wasn't there to send back grains of rice he'd already paid for.

The only excesses were his trips to Paris, taken as a sort of title on investment. Jean had three daughters to marry off, and the back-and-forth between the two continents increased the chances of a good marriage. Besides, accommodation in Paris was free. The family stayed in the house of Jean's brother, Jacques Bouquier, who also owned a bookstore. A favor that Jean never had to repay. 'No, brother, you don't want to expose your family to the dangers of Brazil. Rio is a filthy place, with fetid alleys full of stale air. When a breeze does arrive, it's only to spread mysterious illnesses that wipe out foreigners. A true horror!' he would say.

It wasn't exactly a romance that occurred between Isabelle and Antonio. It was a spark, lit one rainy Wednesday when the girl was instructed by Eulália to look for a notepad with Antonio in the stockroom. 'Those in the window have faded in the sun, show the young lady the new models that arrived last week. Tinoco put them on the shelf in the back,' Eulália said.

The stockroom's single lamp was not bright enough to illuminate the entire space, and the noise of the rain on the rooftop only increased the sense of seclusion. As Antonio showed his client the pile of notepads, Isabelle's arm touched his, and never stopped touching it. Antonio felt his stomach do a somersault and a wave of heat climb up his neck. Seconds later the heat flash became a terrible itch, one of those that nails can't resolve. What Isabelle felt remains a mystery. During that infinite moment in which their arms touched the young woman continued looking at the block of notepads with a peculiar sort of interest, as though it were the military band playing in the park, or an opera at the municipal theater.

Antonio didn't have time to ask himself why his stomach was doing a somersault, or why his neck itched so much. Isabelle also could not hear her father's complaining, for he would certainly protest the purchase of a notepad given there was so much paper at home.

The day after the touching of arms, Jean Bouquier suffered a stroke that left him paralyzed on the left side of his body. When he understood it was necessary to hire a manager for the bookstore, that he would have to pay for the doctor visits, for the vials of medicine and the nurses, he did the math and thought it a better deal to die.

His widow and daughters wailed throughout the funeral. They were tears of rage. Jean Bouquier left his fortune to his brother, and just a few *contos de réis* to his wife. Now she would have to make her own decisions. Beginning with the choice of whether to spend the inheritance on five years of life without want, like the rich woman she had been until then, but who hadn't yet had the chance to really enjoy life. Or to use the money to live the rest of her days frugally, like the years she'd spent with her husband.

When Isabelle arrived with red eyes in the stationery store, the news of the death and the will of Jean Bouquier had already made the rounds through the neighborhood. Dona Eulália didn't have a trace of French on her lips and the girl understood that she would never return to seek out a notepad in the stockroom.

Time passed. Antonio's neck was cured of the wounds caused by the itching. His teeth yellowed, his chest was soon void of muscle. Some of the houses in Tijuca were demolished and gave way to small buildings three stories high. Dona Eulália left her post behind the cash register to spend her days seated next to the radio.

One Friday afternoon Eulália appeared in the stationery store with a red-headed young woman wearing a dress of ivory-colored silk and fat pearl earrings.

'Antonio, look who's here. Henriqueta!'

Henriqueta was a distant cousin on his father's side. So distant, in fact, that her side of the family still had some money. She had short hair, narrow eyes, and an awkward smile, the kind that asks permission to express itself.

'You remember Henriqueta, *don't you*? From the house in Glória, where we used to spend Christmas? From the picnic along the Trail of the Silk-Cotton Trees where we celebrated your brother's birthday? *You remember, don't you?*'

Antonio didn't remember the picnic. But he remembered a Christmas tree that touched the ceiling of a huge salon, his father intercepting the waiters serving champagne, and a girl who was taller than him, who kicked his shins with her orthopedic boots.

During the ensuing decades, Henriqueta had corrected her flat feet and developed into a pretty young woman. Her prettiness should have disappeared already; in those times prettiness was not something that women kept after the age of thirty. But Henriqueta was one of the rare women of that time who refused to grow old, retaining a certain youth in her face uncommon for her age. She had everything she needed to be happy, but she was desperate. She regretted having been too choosy at a time when women shouldn't have that luxury. She had spent her youth refusing fiancés. One was too tall, another was too short, the other was too ugly, another even uglier, and all of them – all of them – too boring. She discarded each one in turn, and when two or three white hairs appeared on her head they discarded her.

Faced with the possibility of spending the rest of her life like her two unmarried aunts, who filled their days with arguments and egg custard, Henriqueta's independent streak was broken. She got it in her head that she needed to marry, or else she wasn't Henriqueta Castro Lima. And exactly because she was Henriqueta *Castro Lima*, she knew it wouldn't be difficult to acquire a husband. She had a coat of arms in her pocket, an inheritance in the bank, and an enormous desire to be happy. She would find her companion, and she knew she would be able to fall in love with the man her money could buy.

True love was what existed at the moment between Eulália and Henriqueta. It seemed Antonio's cousin was in need of a cozy nest. She abandoned the enormous salons of her mansion to spend whole afternoons in the tiny living room in Antonio's apartment. Even from the hall he could hear the chuckles the two shared. He would arrive home to find empty coffee cups and cake crumbs on the center table.

During the long talks between the women, many ancestors were brought back to life. Beginning with Onofre the

Useless, who was redeemed from his ethylic sins and raised to the position of a fated martyr. It wasn't for a lack of character but an excess of adversities that his life ended amid distilled beverages. The two women spent many hours trying to discover links between them to justify the long afternoons spent talking. But the only link was he who opened the door at quarter past six each afternoon, who kept his head down after saying goodnight, and who walked to his room in silence.

'Antonio, son, come sit with us!'

He would thank her for the invitation but reply that he was busy. He needed to add some new stamps, recently arrived from overseas, to his collection. He only left the bedroom when the living room fell quiet, and to listen to the praise showered on his cousin Henriqueta during dinner. She had traveled the world, and had a house in Petrópolis. She had studied in Porto, and had a Ford 1934.

Antonio's discomfort only grew. He would leave his spoon on the table to relieve himself of an itch that began at his waist, climbed up through his chest, and settled on his back.

Antonio lost a lot of weight during those weeks. He frequently abandoned his dinner halfway through, pulling off strips of skin from his neck. Dona Eulália raised her eyes to the heavens and asked the Virgin Mary to relieve his discomfort, and then lowered them again to prepare the mixture of Minancora cream and cornstarch that she applied to her son's wounds. Later she switched the cornstarch for talcum powder, and then the talcum powder for wheat flour. The wheat flour for Rugol cream, the Rugol cream for Leite de Rosas moisturizer, and the Leite de Rosas for an emulsion of camphor oil with cornmeal.

One March afternoon, Henriqueta was in the living room with Eulália when the Tijuca sky grew dark. The rains everyone had been waiting for all month were ready to fall in a single downpour. Henriqueta jumped to her feet with fright, Eulália told her to sit down. Imagine if she let the young woman leave at a time like that, when the streets were about to become rivers. Henriqueta insisted on leaving, Eulália insisted she stay, and after just a few minutes of this game they both knew that the guest wouldn't be going anywhere.

'You'll eat dinner with us today.'

It was the perfect opportunity to turn the affair into a love triangle. But candles were lit only because the electricity failed. The dinner was for two only because Eulália announced she had a headache. And the man on the other side of the table was there only because he had to be. Henriqueta understood all this very quickly. As quick as the lightning rods that lit up the living room and her cousin, who never took his hands off his neck. She rose from the table, walked up to Antonio, and kissed his cheek. A kiss that didn't cause Antonio any excitement. It was as if he was being kissed by a sister.

The following day the wounds on Antonio's neck began to heal. A few weeks later, Henriqueta took a ship to New York, where she intended to spend a few months. She had heard that in that city, women over thirty lived as though they were forever twenty years old. She never returned to Brazil.

In the years that followed, mother and son would lead a peaceful existence. Eulália with her radio and her medicines, Antonio with his papers and Euridice. Euridice, whom he followed from afar and admired so much, and who, he accepted tranquilly, would never be his.

Everything changed that winter. Antonio began to stutter before Guida, and Eulália's health began to worsen again. Her blood pressure fell, her blood sugar rose – and how was it possible to live with that strange noise coming from her intestine? Her days were numbered.

'Take advantage of the little time I have left,' she would say to Antonio from beneath the covers.

That was a half-truth, since no one's day of death appears on the calendar. Or perhaps it's better said that it was a half-lie. There were two things that Eulália had no intention of ever doing. One was to die. The other was to allow her son to marry a bride she hadn't chosen.

But Antonio, perhaps for having tired of his mother the professional complainer, perhaps because he needed something beyond stamps and stationery, stopped listening to Eulália with two ears and an open heart. He took her temperature, measured her blood pressure, doled out her medicine, and cooked her rice without salt, without season-ing, without fat, and almost without rice, so frugal was he. Then he would wash his hands, change his clothes, and go out dressed up to the nines to meet Guida.

Guida Gusmao. Who was that woman? She was sister to Euridice, the woman Eulália had never liked, but who she had never taken the time to sniff out, because married women gave off no odors capable of waking Eulália's nose. She had never seen the young woman but had received detailed reports from her friend Zélia. Guida painted her nails red and had a teenage son. She wore make-up even to go to the open-air market and never stepped foot in a church. She walked about with her breast fuller than a Christmas turkey, as though it were bigger even than herself, and certainly bigger than that of the other women in the neigh-borhood. She was as affected as her sister, only in a different way. Euridice was affected because she enjoyed living in her world, and Guida was affected because she enjoyed being the most beautiful in our world.

Guida was an adversary worthy of Eulália's bitterness. *If this Guida thinks she's going to have anything to do with my Antonio beyond long walks she's got another think coming*, Eulália would spend her days saying to herself. *Antonio will never leave me, he will never leave this apartment*, Eulália repeated to herself.

Eulália's mantra was similar to another, this one coming from a few blocks up the street. Guida had already taken note of Eulália's plans for domination but was certain that one day Antonio would be hers. 'He's going to be mine, all mine,' she would say. 'Mine alone,' she repeated.

It wasn't long before Eulália's illnesses worsened and Guida's charms multiplied. One night, soon after that exchange of practicalities at the Colombo cafe, Guida and Antonio were out sharing a fondue in a candlelit restaurant when the waiter interrupted the couple.

'Senhor Antonio Lacerda?'

'Yes.'

'It's your mother on the telephone.'

'The end is nigh, the end is nigh,' Eulália cried at the other end of the line. 'I'm full of chest spasms, I don't know how to breathe anymore. I only have a few hours left, or minutes – minutes! Come see me one last time, and call the priest to administer extreme unction.'

Antonio flew through stoplights, barreled into the sacristy to wake the priest, flew up to the apartment three steps at a time, and found his mother knitting on the sofa.

'I could have died of emphysema,' she said without looking up.

While Eulália nearly died once a month, Guida became younger and more beautiful with each day. Her breasts looked as though they wouldn't fit inside her dresses. Her legs grew even longer, and her smiles grew so much wider that whenever he looked at that little space between her teeth, Antonio even forgot about Euridice. These moments of amnesia grew more and more common in proportion to the degree that Guida showed Antonio the true meaning of life, which he discovered was connected to the undoing of the clasps of a bra.

There with those breasts – and those legs, and that rear – Antonio forgot about Euridice, forgot about his mother, forgot about the itching. When Guida began to talk practicalities, using words like *commitment*, and Antonio changed the subject, Guida denied him access to those parts of her body, and the man went wild. He forgot even more things, like the terrible consequences of asking Guida to marry him. The words gushed forth from his mouth, leaving him full of both regret and relief.

'Yes, yes, yes!' Guida replied, toppling on to the poor man with a hug.

She was a winner.

After Guida said *yes yes yes* she furrowed her brow. She was still married to Marcos, and to commit to another man she needed first to request the dissolution of their marriage.

In the years that followed her abandonment she had spent hours going over every minute of her marriage, trying to find some sign that she had done something wrong, or many things wrong, to make her husband run away like that. She never found a reason and always arrived at the same conclusion: besides being an asshole, a creep, a maggot, and a good-for-nothing, Marcos was a weak and ill-prepared individual, and for this he deserved the nickname Sissy.

Marcos the Sissy, she understood, was in no condition to lead an independent life. He had returned to Botafogo. *He must have been behind the velvet curtains when I showed up at the house looking for him*, Guida thought to herself. That was the truth. Marcos was behind the curtains, and he stayed there as Guida received the news from the doorman that he hadn't returned to his parents' house. When the young woman had made it halfway back to the trolley station, Marcos pulled back the curtain. He had the impression he saw Guida slightly doubled over, and for a few seconds thought about running to protect her. The seconds passed, and Marcos decided to have a coffee.

If he had returned to the mansion in Botafogo, it was to the mansion that Guida ought to address the letter requesting the dissolution of their marriage. She thought long and hard about what to write, but every time she thought she'd had a good idea it lost its meaning when she tried to put it to paper. She decided to write only what was necessary: 'I want to sign papers to dissolve our marriage.' It was all that needed to be said.

But as soon as she picked up the pen to write it, Guida was overtaken with an unusual eloquence and filled four leaves of office paper with the speed of a medium. She unloaded everything – the hardships she'd suffered, her husband's lack of manliness, the tough years in Estácio. She saved the news of their child for the climax. 'His name is Francisco Gusmao. He has inherited your eyes, but nothing else.'

Guida's letter arrived just in time. Marcos was also look-ing for her, for the very same reason. He wanted to make official his union with a second cousin named Maria Ester.

Some weeks later, Marcos and Guida met to sign the papers in front of a judge. It was, in reality, a non-meeting. Marcos saw from the room the contours of his ex-wife and directed his gaze to everything but Guida. Guida only took her eyes off the judge to sign the documents. When Marcos grabbed the pen, it still carried the warmth of Guida's hand. He trembled as he signed his name.

After the dissolution, Marcos went to live in his second cousin's apartment. It was a penthouse in Copacabana with art nouveau gates, which gave the young man the impres-sion he was in prison. Perhaps it was hormones, perhaps it was nerves, perhaps it was the new responsibilities of a life together. The fact is that Maria Ester changed drastically after the marriage. She let her mustache grow, began to burp out loud, and sat just like Buddha amid the sofa cush-ions, ordering around the maid and her husband. Marcos's only consolation was to spend time out of the house. His father arranged a job for him in government that required absolutely nothing from him. He passed his free hours in an office downtown, looking at his notebook and redrawing the lines for his games of tic-tac-toe. Every now and then, he thought about the son he would never see, calculating his age without knowing whether he was doing the math in order to imagine his son, or the time he had spent away from Guida.

Guida, for her part, needed to tell Antonio about Marcos. She spent days wringing her hands and walking from one side of the bedroom to the other, trying to determine the best way to reveal the truth but finding no response in any of the walls against which she almost banged her head every few seconds. She asked Euridice for advice, and her sister ended her agony with a single phrase: 'The best way of telling the truth is to tell the truth.'

One Thursday morning, Guida took Chico to school. Then she walked to the stationery store, to speak with her fiancé. The worry in the young woman's eyes made Antonio send his assistant Tinoco home early and lock the door to the store, displaying a sign that read *Back soon.*

The two of them sat in the back of the store. It was while looking at the floor and wringing her hands that Guida told Antonio the truth. Yes, she had been a wild, crazy child: she had fled home at the most tender of ages to marry a man who had sold himself as a good provider. This good provider was nothing more than an opportunist who abandoned Guida with her son still in her womb, leaving a trail of destruction that began in her heart and extended to all the material comforts stolen from the daily life of the young single mother and her tender child. She had to support her new family on her own, and that's how she came to work behind the cash register at a haberdashery in Rio Comprido.

Guida raised her eyes and looked straight at her boyfriend.

'And that's why, my love, we cannot marry. I was already married; I can't commit myself again. I promise to be your devoted companion for the rest of my days. But we can never step foot in a church or before a justice of the peace.'

Antonio's face relaxed the more Guida spoke. The woman he loved could never, ever, marry him. They would never have a formal commitment. He wouldn't have to sign papers, he wouldn't have to make promises in front of a judge. He wouldn't have to hear the implicit threats in the priest's homily, when the holy man said that what God brings together can never, ever, be undone for the rest of our lives. For the first time in weeks he no longer felt a terrible itch. He took Guida's hands and with the widest smile he'd ever given he said that yes, he agreed to never marry her. They embraced and Guida didn't mind dirtying her face with the cornmeal plaster that Antonio wore on his neck and which no longer had any use.

In May of that year, Antonio and Guida announced to the neighborhood that they would marry. They would take their vows in Portugal, according to the wishes of Guida's grandmother. It seemed this grandmother was a very religious woman, who had once knelt for months on end, rubbing her knees raw as she asked the Virgin Mary for a second husband for her granddaughter, one as good as the first had been. Now that her request had been granted it was necessary to carry out the marriage in the city of Fátima, named for Our Lady to whom Guida's grandmother was devoted.

The trip to Portugal went through a series of changes, none of them announced by Antonio and Guida. They traded Europe for Brazil's countryside, and the ceremony in a church for two weeks in a hotel. They barely left the bedroom, so there was no need to worry about a possible encounter with anyone they knew.

Not everyone in the neighborhood believed the story they'd told. Some women expressed surprise upon discovering the matchmaking capabilities of Our Lady of Fátima, who had up until that point shown more concern for the great questions facing humanity, like an end to war, or the Day of Judgment. Others were suspicious about a wedding without guests – not even Antonio's mother could be present. Many of them were indignant at the groom's cruelty. How could a forty-nine-year-old man abandon his mother for so many days, leaving her to the care of two nurses who worked in shifts so that she was never alone?

There were many questions in those days, but no one in the neighborhood managed to disprove the story told by Antonio and Guida. They did arrive at a consensus on one thing: the enormous ring Guida wore on her left hand was made of solid gold.

CHAPTER 12

No one knows for sure what came first. These were facts that were blurred over time and space, and later were diluted in the memory of the participants. One witness would say it happened like this, another would say it happened like that, and the only consensus was that the events did in fact take place.

And this is what occurred: Antenor passed all tests of resistance, ability, and political maneuvers thrown at him by the upper brass of the Bank of Brazil. His desk went through transformations imperceptible to the naked eye but visible after some years. It gradually grew bigger and moved to areas with wide-open spaces near large windows.

After decades of dedication and advancement he landed at a desk in an office of his own, which received the early morning sun through the five neoclassic windows of the bank headquarters. A smaller office, occupied by a secretary in black stilettos, separated Antenor from the other public servants, who at this point were more public than he was.

Antenor's promotion to vice-president hadn't been big news in itself. He had always believed he was predestined to occupy a leather chair in a room decorated with Persian rugs. That appeared to be the natural order of things. He was merely following the river current, a river that had never had any undertows, since the day he'd begun memorizing his multiplication tables.

It was around this time that Antenor began to think he knew everything. The best shoes were to be found at Casa Aguiar, a GE radio was better than an Emerson. Minancora cream was good for anything and Leite de Rosas was useless. It didn't matter what anyone else said, their words were transformed into a buzz later interrupted by Antenor, who would say, 'Don't interrupt me! GE is better because that's how it is.' Afonso was an excellent student, Antenor knew this. It was the grades he received that were incorrect. Cecilia was an exemplary young lady whose lipstick was smudged because a friend had bumped up against her face. Euridice was a fulfilled woman absent of worries, thanks to him, Antenor, who never allowed the spoon to touch the bottom of the food jars. They had always had abundance, they would always have stability, and for that reason, his wife was happy.

Euridice's eyes wandered until they landed on her husband. He was a lost cause. Later they simply wandered, as she sat in front of the bookshelf. The woman's melancholy state, which had improved with her sister's presence, worsened when Guida went to live with Antonio. The house fell silent once more, and once again there were more hours in the day than there ought to be. Antenor had work, Maria had her cleaning, her children had their whole lives. And Euridice, what did she have?

Afternoons in the living room, facing the bookshelf. Now and then Maria poked her head out of the kitchen to look at her boss, her feet stretching out over her slippers, arms resting across her belly, a wooden spoon lolling from one hand. Euridice didn't even notice, or pretended not to notice. The maid would walk back into the kitchen, shaking her head. When Cecilia and Afonso arrived, Euridice pretended not to see, looking from side to side. When Antenor arrived, she pretended even harder. She didn't want to give her husband explanations.

Perhaps it had been the repetition. Years and years seated in the same place, facing the emptiness embodied by the bookshelf. Or perhaps it happened because it was meant to. The fact is that during that new season of empty gazes, Euridice began to feel different. It was a weak sensation in the beginning, almost like an itch. She noticed that it only appeared when she sat there in the same place, eyes fixed on the same spot.

Euridice began to sit at her post less to gaze at the nothingness and more to wait for that sensation to arrive. The sensation would appear, and in the midst of the silence it found room to grow. It grew until Euridice could see it, and

Euridice saw that the sensation was exactly that: the sensation was the gift of observation.

Euridice could *see* the bookshelf for the bookshelf.

She saw the bookshelf.

She rose to her feet and passed her right hand along the spines of the books. Dostoevsky, Tolstoy, Flaubert. Gilberto Freyre, Caio Prado Jr., Antonio Candido. Virginia Woolf and George Eliot, Simone de Beauvoir and Jane Austen. Machado de Assis and Lima Barreto, Hemingway and Steinbeck. Some of those books she had read and already forgotten, others she had bought and forgotten to read. A few others were added by Antenor, who bought books the same way others buy light bulbs: they are always good to have around, just in case.

It was a decent library. She sat back down on the sofa in the company of a book, and for the first time in a long time she directed her full attention to the pages before her. Later she grabbed another, and another, and began connecting the imaginary dots that made all of those texts one.

When she'd finished reading, Euridice put on one of her dresses and went downtown to buy a typewriter. Returning home, she cleared some space on the desk in the study that had until then been Antenor's. She sent Maria to find another place for the accounting texts her husband had stubbornly held on to since he'd turned eighteen. She placed the typewriter on the desk and spent the rest of the afternoon exploring the letters. *Tack-tack-tack is lovely on the ears*, Maria thought to herself. As long as the sound could be heard, no one in the house would sit staring at the bookshelf.

Tack-tack-tack was the sound that defined those times. In the beginning, the sounds came out more slowly, a *tack* here and a *tack* there. Later they were transformed into a constant noise, a *tack-tack-tack-tack-tack* that filled the entire afternoon, so constant that its noise became nearly imperceptible.

Beyond writing, Euridice found herself another function for her hands, which was to light the cigarettes she would sneak into the first-floor bathroom. Each cigarette was a cry of freedom that was complete in itself and left no tracks. She soon had yellow teeth, and breath full of mint mixed with something Antenor couldn't quite identify. She also acquired a sure expression, which came from the combination of the puffs of smoke and the books she read.

The only person who knew about her cigarettes was Maria. She saw her boss lock herself in the bathroom, smelled the cigarette smoke leaving the ventilation window, and heard the sprays of perfume Euridice launched into the air, to fool herself into thinking she had fooled Maria. The maid couldn't have cared less. In fact, she thought that it had taken a long time for Don'Euridice to find a form of escape. When she herself was upset about something – for instance, *my hus-band showed up, stole our money, and began whacking the children with the broom* – she used the bottles from Antenor's bar to alleviate her frustrations. Maria avoided the Ballantine's – she knew Antenor continued drinking it during the Nights of Whiskey and Weeping – and instead explored the liquors that sat there like statues. When the alcohol in the bottle became low, she would replenish it with water and sugar so Antenor wouldn't take notice, and life would continue, easier to face.

As soon as Euridice heard the front door open when the children returned from school she would remove the sheet of paper from the typewriter and lock it away with the others in the desk drawer. Then she would go to the living room and ask her children how their day had been.

'It was good,' Afonso would say.

'I got a B on my math test,' Cecilia announced one time. 'The teacher said if I keep it up, I'm not going to have any trouble passing my college entrance exams. Luiza showed up with a French manicure. She said there's a salon on Rua Mariz e Barros that does them that way. Can you buy me the new Tom Jobim album? I really want it.'

Antenor would arrive soon thereafter. He kissed his wife on the forehead, went to the bedroom to change his clothes, came back to the living room in his slippers. The family ate dinner together, one of them asking to pass the rice bowl, the other commenting on how hot it was that day.

Everyone knew about Euridice's new routine but no one dared ask what she was writing so much about. It was on an October night, when Euridice had already progressed quite far with her writing, that she let slip, between one forkful and another, the bit of information that sated the family's curiosity.

'I'm writing a book. It's about the history of invisibility.'

Everyone continued eating in silence. No one bothered to ask any more about the book, if she wanted to publish it, what it was about, or who she was to decide to write just like that. They all held the conviction that Euridice was only to be taken seriously when announcing that dinner was ready or that it was time to wake up for school. Her projects were confined to the universe of that house. Or perhaps that of the neighborhood, if the project in question was making cheese sandwiches for a birthday party.

Euridice didn't let herself worry. This *not worrying* was part of her new phase. She spent her days locked in the study, and if the sound of the typewriter fell silent, it was because books were lying open over the desk, with Euridice's head square in between them. Now and then Maria heard some-one talking and poked her head out of the kitchen to see if the visitor wanted a coffee. When she made it to the living room she would find Euridice talking to herself, behind the study door. She would let out a sigh before returning to the kitchen.

It was with her books that Euridice conversed. 'This here seems brilliant, I can't agree with this argument, this paragraph has everything to do with this other book, just look,' she would say, addressing the pages before her. She underlined passages, wrote in the margins, and sometimes abused the exclamation point.

Now and then Euridice would catch the bus to the National Library. She would open the archive catalog, jot down a few numbers, and spend the day between stacks of books. She made notes in a new ruled notebook that Antonio was only too happy to sell her. Late in the afternoon she would return home, walking to the bus stop and clearing a path between the famished pigeons in the square in front of the library. But she saw neither the pigeons, the path, nor the bus. Euridice could only see the words that she'd read, as she looked distractedly through the bus window.

The only one who seemed to understand Euridice's eccentricities was Chico. During Sunday lunches, when the Gusmao-Campelos welcomed Guida, Antonio, Chico, and Eulália into their home (this last one only appeared when she wasn't sick, and she was never sick when Euridice was making salt cod), Chico went up to the study with his aunt. No one heard much of their conversations because they were conducted behind closed doors, and because no one was all that interested.

What caused consternation during Euridice's new phase was her expression: that gaze of hers now seemed to pierce right through people, as though stealing their secrets. But as long as the household routine was maintained, as long as Afonso got a haircut and his uniform was clean, as long as Cecilia's skirt was the right length and she didn't laugh too loud, as long as Antenor's slippers and the couch pillows were in the right place, Euridice could have whatever look on her face she very well pleased.

The Gusmao-Campelos had a life that was normal at last.

But that isn't the full truth.

It's nearly the full truth.

Antenor was still engaged in his mission to become a cuckold. He still drank more than he ought to on the Nights of Whiskey and Weeping, he continued to blame his wife for her nights of lust prior to their wedding. 'Who was he?' Antenor would ask, and Euridice would always respond that *he* never existed. But now she'd come to think that such nights would have been a good thing, for her and for Antenor.

Guida was present on one of those drinking nights. She sent Maria home as soon as she heard Antenor start to yell and did the dishes herself. She was drying the plates when Euridice appeared in the kitchen doorway, head hung low.

'Antenor does these things. He thinks I wasn't a virgin when we married because I didn't bleed that first night.'

Guida continued drying the dishes.

'That happened to me, too.'

'What?'

'The same thing happened to me. There wasn't any stain on the sheet, but Marcos didn't much care.' She stopped for a second, looked straight ahead. 'We were so in love in those days.'

Euridice eyed her sister the same way she eyed an interesting book. Then she went to put the silverware away.

Euridice's writings lay in the desk drawer, stacked serenely in the darkness. The sunlight only snuck in once a day, when Euridice opened the drawer to add the pages she'd just written. There was hardly any noise, besides that of the typewriter. Despite the quietness of that life, those seemingly harmless pages had the near-magic power granted to certain sheets of paper: that of being able to disturb a great many people.

These great many people disturbed by Euridice's writing were the other women in the neighborhood. In the minds of Zélia's followers, Euridice's latest antics went beyond boldness – they were an insult. Who was she to read difficult authors and write down anything besides cake recipes?

Euridice was disrespecting one of the basic principles of the Neighbor Statute, which stated that the happiness of a group is only possible when everyone in this group is alike, from the size of their bank account to their aspirations.

Upon learning from Zélia that the *tack-tack-tack* was the sound of Euridice's typewriter, and seeing Euridice walking through the neighborhood with her arms wrapped around a stack of books, the Corporation of Women of the Environs of Rua Uruguai felt as though they'd taken a direct hit. Euridice's behavior displayed an arrogance that could only be explained by a loss of reason.

The evidence of her dementia was ample: she no longer respected the laws of morality and good sense by continuing to greet Silvia after her separation. She didn't want to participate in the Tijuca Council against Communism, founded by Dona Agnes. Euridice refused an invitation to become treasurer of the philanthropic committee of the América Football Club, engaged in eradicating poverty worldwide through the production of crocheted shoes for the bare feet of the black children who lived in the Borel slum.

One time Dona Efigenia asked Euridice what she was carrying in her bag from the Da Vinci bookstore, and Euridice had the nerve to tell her she'd bought the *Complete Works* of William Shakespeare and an *Oxford English Dictionary*, *because she thought Shakespeare ought to be read in its original language.*

Poor Euridice, the neighbors lamented. Now she'd lost it in two languages. They all felt such pity for the woman. When she began to wear a sea-green turban, they were filled with happiness because they could redouble their pity. Euridice no longer bothered with her appearance. She didn't bother spending an hour in front of the dressing table, or two inside those mushroom caps in the beauty salons, just to parade through the neighborhood with her beehive, the kind that made a person look like she'd rolled up a camisole, stuck it on the crown of her head and covered the whole thing with hair.

It was shortly thereafter that everything changed. A truck rolled up in front of the Gusmao-Campelo household. Men in overalls walked out holding boxes, and more men in overalls with even more boxes. The bystanders couldn't do anything but keep watching and begin to feel their blood boil.

It took Zélia an hour and a half to send out her first report. Antenor was all nerves as he watched the package containing his TV, Euridice was transfixed by the package of dishes, the delivery men were focused on developing hernias by carrying so many boxes full of Euridice's books.

Yes, they were moving, Zélia said. And where were they going?

Zélia did her best to hide her face full of disappointment. 'To Ipanema.'

To move to Ipanema in the early sixties was not merely to shift one's residence by a few kilometers. It was to pass through time portals, to live in a place that made the rest of Rio look like the past. Ipanema was a neighborhood full of writers, poets, and musicians. Actors, painters, sculptors. Journalists, dramaturges, and cinema directors. Ipanema was also a family neighborhood, full of houses surrounded by low walls, buildings only a few stories high, and comfortable apartments that occupied entire floors, the most expensive in Rio.

It was to one of those apartments that Euridice and Antenor moved. Six living-room windows framed the Atlantic Ocean, the extensive hallway led to four rooms with built-in closets and a view overlooking the tops of the almond trees.

The move confirmed the neighbors' suspicions, prompted by the Gusmao-Campelos' abundance of domestic appliances: the family had become rich. They were no longer subject to the rules of Tijuca's middle class, and a new evaluation was made of Euridice. She was not, in fact, nuts. Euridice was an exotic creature. Exotic with her turban, exotic with her writing. Exotic because there were no longer any parameters on which to base a comparison.

Euridice left Tijuca without looking back. She wanted nothing more from the neighborhood, not even the dust left behind on her shoes. When the boxes were loaded in the truck, she climbed into the family car and they made their way to Ipanema. Antenor pulled out into the street and Euridice crossed her arms in one big *up-yours*, though she swears to this day that she was only using her left hand to toss the wrapper for her cough drop out the window.

Ipanema, she would soon discover, also had its Zélias. But it was a new neighborhood and she was a new Euridice. And that, she knew, made all the difference.

CHAPTER 13

After her marriage to Antonio, Guida faced yet another challenge: her mother-in-law's idle moments. These moments were composed of all the seconds of all the minutes of all the hours of the day, and were used only to make Guida's life a living hell. Dona Eulália hadn't accepted the fury of initiative that had befallen Antonio, *her* Antonio, a boy who for half a century had behaved so well. His marriage to Guida was a blow that compromised her health but also served to make her immortal. Eulália promised herself that in order for Antonio and Guida to stay together they would have to do so over her dead body, and dying had never been in her plans.

In the beginning, Guida did what she could to please Eulália. The bath was cold? She filled the bathtub with hot water. It was too hot? She tossed in a bucket of cold water. Now it was just a bit cold? She threw in some more hot water.

Now it was just a bit hot? She tossed in some cold water. Guida's resilience frustrated Eulália, since she could hardly complain about the bathwater being wet. The beans had too much broth? Guida would heat up the pan so the water would evaporate. Now they were too thick? Guida would add more water. It was the seasoning that was wrong, and Guida stood next to Eulália, taking orders to add garlic and olive oil. If she had been able, she would have counted out the grains of salt to add exactly the number her mother-in-law wanted.

She soon understood that she couldn't count all the grains of salt every time Eulália made a demand. It was the bath, the beans, the way she ironed and folded the clothes. How she arranged the food in the refrigerator and the invisible layer of dust lingering in the house.

So Guida appealed to the heavens. The woman would light a candle every seven days in the apartment bathroom and pray for a solution – to Jesus Christ our Lord; to Saint Sebastian of Rio de Janeiro; to Saint Anthony, the Wonder Worker; to Saint Rita, Patron Saint of the Impossible – while Dona Eulália pounded on the bathroom door, telling her daughter-in-law that she had to come out that instant because she had a urinary-tract infection and couldn't go more than five minutes without using the toilet.

The only effect the candles had was to turn the bathroom ceiling black. It was Chico, not some saint, who consoled Guida in the evenings when Eulália laid it on thick with her criticisms. 'It will get better, Mom,' he would say, just to say it.

In the following months, Dona Eulália's urinary-tract infection grew worse. She couldn't so much as make her way to the bathroom without relieving herself in the hallway. Guida would clean the floor, change her mother-in-law's clothing, and settle her on the sofa. She washed Eulália's panties in the sink and then walked back to the living room, just in time to be told that she was using too much water.

Life-or-death moments were common on weekend evenings. Eulália would agonize when she heard the first notes of 'Bésame Mucho' coming from the dark living room. 'The end is nigh, the end is nigh!' Eulália would scream from the bedroom, and Antonio would run to the bedroom only to see once again that his mother was not dying. Guida would turn on the light and cross her arms. She tapped her foot to the sound of the bolero, waiting for her husband to return. The song would come to an end with Antonio still in his mother's bedroom.

When her mother-in-law began to unload her intestines in places other than the bathroom, Guida decided to speak to Antonio. Dona Eulália seemed very sick, wouldn't it be better to take her to an old folks' home, so that she could receive specialized care from capable professionals?

Antonio stared at Guida as though she had antennas growing out of her head. He would never abandon his mother. How could he sleep knowing that the woman who had dedicated her whole life to him was in the company of strangers, that she could die at any moment, and that he, only he, was responsible for such cruelty?

Guida stared at her husband like someone recently cured of myopia. Antonio would always be tethered to his mother. The umbilical cord had been cut at birth, a time which her mother-in-law had had the terrible gall to survive. But in her husband's head, the cord would never, ever be severed.

Guida spent the next morning lost in unprecedented thoughts, while her mother-in-law sucked on sweet coconut balls in front of the television. Any truce between the two would only be possible through death. If their dispute took into account the number of years lived, Guida would hold the advantage. But if it took into account the comparative resistance of the two parties, Eulália would be the victor.

Guida soon found herself thinking about something that she didn't really want to think about, but which began to pass through her head. It was as though she'd heard a summons, which she still swears she never did. And since this something neither passed fully through her head nor was banished, it soon put down roots. Guida didn't much like to think about this something but she also didn't do anything to stop thinking about it. It was, in reality, a hypothesis, an idea, something that could happen. But if someone were to ask her if this hypothesis would one day come to pass, she would say no way, that would never happen. And that something was the following: *What if I were to kill my mother-in-law?*

She began to look at Dona Eulália with renewed interest. In the morning, the old woman drank her coffee together with eight pills. She complained about the crumbs on the table, or the sun creeping through the window. Later she turned on the radio or sat in front of the TV, eating sweet coconut balls. She would complain about the lack of light ('Why on earth did Guida close the shutters?'), about the noise made by the steaks in the frying pan, and about her favorite sofa pillow lying so far away, there on the other end of the couch. She lunched at noon in the company of eleven pills. She complained about the dessert – 'Jell-O again? Give me a real dessert, my time here is short. Pudding on a Tuesday? Do you want me to die of diabetes?'

In the afternoons, Dona Eulália alternated her TV programs with long periods spent in front of the window eating sweet coconut balls. She only abandoned her post to go to the bathroom. 'What a smelly bathroom, Guida. What are you using to clean this place, wishful thinking?' She would eat dinner at six, accompanied by nine pills and complaints about the seasoning of the steak.

That's how things stood – Guida with the idea in her head which wasn't hers, and Dona Eulália as the sovereign queen and occasional dying mother – when one Wednesday afternoon a black woman passed through the street peddling sweets.

'Do you have any toffee?' Dona Eulália yelled from the window.

'I sure do, ma'am,' the black woman responded, and Dona Eulália sent Guida down to buy some.

Guida came back with the toffee and went to the kitchen to grab a serving plate. 'That will only dirty the plates,' Eulália said.

The younger woman sighed – in those days, Guida never breathed, she only sighed – and went to the kitchen to season the beans with three garlic cloves, half a chopped onion, three spoons of olive oil and two pinches of salt, according to her mother-in-law's instructions. She could hear a smacking sound coming from Eulália's mouth as she ate the toffee. *Smack, smack. Smack, smack. Smack, smack.*

That was when the idea that wasn't exactly Guida's returned, and everything became a bit confusing. Guida began to think that she could make the toffee herself, and could make it all the time, knowing that if she made the toffee her mother-in-law would love it, and knowing that, who knows, perhaps, she would die choking on a piece.

Dona Eulália didn't even bother to criticize the toffee that Guida began to make every morning. The old lady looked like a cocker spaniel, staring at her daughter-in-law with a plea on her face for more. If dentures could develop cavities, Eulália's would have turned black. She spent the whole day making a smacking sound with the roof of her mouth. *Smack, smack. Smack, smack. Smack, smack.* When a larger piece got stuck between her teeth, she stuck her finger in her mouth to dislodge it. When she ate an enormous piece, her dentures shifted out of place, and Eulália popped them back into place with a *krrr-eck. Smack, smack. Krrr-eck. Smack, smack. Smack, smack. Krrr-eck. Smack, smack. Krrr-eck.*

The toffee candies brought a truce between Guida and Eulália. A truce that occurred shortly before the final battle. It all happened on a Tuesday. Guida was preparing steak

Milanese in the kitchen, Dona Eulália was in the living room sucking on a piece of toffee. The *smacks* coming from the living room were as consistent as a metronome. *Smack, smack. Smack, smack. Smack, smack. Krrr-eck. Smack, smack. Smack, smack. Smack, smack. Krrr-eck. Smack, smack. Smack, smack. Smack, smack. Krrr-eck.* Until the living room suddenly grew quiet, and Guida heard something fall to the floor, followed by an *argh, argh, argh*.

That's where the story starts to get fuzzy.

When Guida heard this *argh, argh, argh*, she thought the same thing that you, dear readers, are thinking. But then she thought that it wasn't exactly *that* she was hearing, and decided to toss the three remaining steaks in the flour as she hummed a bossa nova tune. She wasn't sure whether she thought it wasn't happening because it was an implausible hypothesis or if she thought it wasn't happening because she wanted it to happen so much, and for that to happen she would need to toss the remaining steaks in the flour. *Argh, argh, argh*, she heard from the other room. That's when Guida came to her senses and ran to the living room and yes, what she both wanted and didn't want to happen was in fact happening. The picture frames from the table were all over the floor and Dona Eulália's eyes were coming out of her head, toffee lodged in her throat.

Guida became desperate. She stuck her hand full of flour down her mother-in-law's throat, but the toffee wouldn't budge. She threw Eulália's dentures across the room, and nothing. She pounded on her mother-in-law's back, turned the old woman upside down, yelled through the window for help, and went back to pounding on her mother-in-law's back. The toffee stayed put, in some unknown location. She knew she had to find a way to help Dona Eulália breathe again, that she need only cut a hole in her neck for the air to pass, but the only thing she could remember from biology class was that the jugular vein also ran along the neck and that this vein was to be found in a location as mysterious as the toffee.

The neighbors arrived next. Some had the opportunity to slap Eulália's back. Others only saw the body. The ambulance arrived half an hour later.

Guida's tears at her mother-in-law's funeral were genuine. She cried for Antonio, who hiccupped with distress, and who could have been thought of as the only orphan in the entire world with coronary problems and hairs in his ears. The mourning period in the couple's apartment lasted a week. That Saturday night, Guida gave Chico some money to go to the movies and put 'Bésame Mucho' on the record player. That was the night Antonio stopped being an orphan.

Life in Tijuca in the beginning of the 1960s was tranquil, perhaps even too tranquil. It had been months since some young girl had become pregnant and disappeared for a week to have an illegal abortion, or for nine months to give birth to a bastard child. Not a single maid was sent away because her belly grew, left with nothing more than the clothes on her back and the certainty that she would never again find work. Not a single family announced a trip abroad by the man of the house, 'abroad' meaning a trip to the Hotel for Bachelors in Santa Teresa. Zélia became addicted to pulling at her cuticles, she was so bored. That's when she learned of a story that was the Best of the Year, perhaps even the Decade.

At her cousin's invitation, Zélia went to a church festival. At this festival she talked with a friend of a cousin who was married to a watch repairman. This watch repairman had a client who lived in the neighborhood of Muda, and this client had a half-sister, who for her part had another half-sister, who told her a story she had heard from a friend, about a neighbor of hers in Estácio who had vanished in the night. What caused this woman's story to pass from tongue to tongue was the fact that she was as beautiful as she was bold. She was a single mother, who declined her favors to men in need, and who lived with a former prostitute – and who knows what they did together under the same roof. It's said that the former prostitute died a hideous death, perhaps paying for her sins, and that the single mother was a bit too lax when it came to caring for her son, because the boy soon became very sick. It seemed that this single mother performed favors for the owner of the local pharmacy, and that her disappearance was related to the man's trip to the hospital after consuming too much of a laxative that, according to those in the know, was hidden in a chocolate cake, or cornbread muffins, or an egg-white pudding, brought to him by this woman during one of their sinful encounters. To this day, the pharmacy owner clenches his fists at the memory of the woman, whose name was Guida Gusmao.

So it's a family trait, Zélia thought to herself. Euridice wasn't the only slut, immortalized in Antenor's cries. She needed to reveal the truth to all interested parties as soon as possible.

Zélia set to work spreading the news, but even after a week the news hadn't managed to reach the principal targets, Guida and Antonio. After Eulália's death, the new family nucleus wanted nothing to do with social events. Bankrolled by his mother, Chico discovered the pleasures of the cinema while Antonio discovered the pleasures of marriage.

When Zélia showed up at the stationery store, only the black boy Tinoco was to be found behind the cash register.

'Do you know where Senhor Antonio is?'

'He was here just this morning, but said he wasn't feeling well.'

A few weeks later, the members of the new family returned to their routine. They were once again able to pay attention to what was happening around them, opening their eyes and ears to other people's stories, and making it possible to hear from these others the stories about their own family.

It was a Monday morning. Antonio was behind the counter, the black boy Tinoco was dusting off notebooks at the other end of the store. Zélia walked in with eyes full of pity, not worrying in the least about being discreet, asking for half a dozen pencils and more cards for her card index. She launched into Guida's story after a brief 'Good morning,' enriching the report with details that could only have been seen by the flies in the corner of the room. She told of vows of love and impassioned kisses, of pearls and emeralds given in exchange for more vows of love and more impassioned kisses. Zélia became inspired, and began to think that a pharmacist couldn't meet Guida's lustful demands, adding a baker, a fireman, and a car mechanic to the story, when she was cut short by an indignant Antonio.

'And who are you, senhora, to come here and slander my wife?'

'But Senhor Antonio, this wasn't my intention…'

'Get out of my store right now.'

That night Antonio told Guida the story he had heard from Zélia. He sent saliva flying, his eyes popped out of his head, and he ranted and raved about the cruelty in the world.

'A life in Estácio – Estácio! Living with a prostitute, pearl necklaces and emerald rings, how could someone come up with so much slander against you, my nymph?'

Guida took Antonio by the hand and told him he was right; it simply wasn't possible. It was envy, that was the only explanation. Envy over their love, as not everyone could be as happy as they were. She asked Antonio to rest his head against her breast as she caressed him. Antonio looked up at her only once.

'It's all a lie. Right?'

'Of course it is. All a lie.'

Antonio nestled his head against her once again. It was a boy that Guida held in her arms. A boy with white around his temples, who glued his ear to Guida's breast to listen to her heartbeat.

That was how the nasty details invented by Zélia and Senhor Pedro's spitting on Guida became part of a single category, a category of facts that never took place. Also in this category was the jewelry that Guida had never received in return for favors. The coconut cake Guida had made for the pharmacist with twenty-three laxative pills. The many days of hard work in Estácio, and Filomena's nights full of suffering. Left behind there were the critical moments of Chico's illness and the kitchen cupboards without food. None of that existed. Later, in bed with her eyes open and her sleeping husband next to her, Guida thought that was an excellent place to store those years of her past.

CHAPTER 14

That morning was the first in forty years that the green-grocer's didn't open its doors. Inside was Senhor Manuel, collapsed on the floor and surrounded by the oranges on which he'd tried to support himself when he felt the first signs of a stroke. The stroke paralyzed the right side of his body and left him with an expression even grumpier than the one he'd assumed after his wife's death.

The old Portuguese man soon discovered that the worst consequence of his stroke wasn't the loss of movement but the lack of control over his fate. If before it had been Senhor Manuel who had laid down the rules, now it was his daughters who ordered him around. The two of them decided (in some fantasy world, in his opinion) that from then on, Guida would take care of their father.

His contorted face didn't look so bad after all, he began to think. Manuel had no plans to exchange anything but a few grunts with his daughter. Guida, for her part, did her best to muffle her own grunts. The old man in the bed was responsible for so many years of suffering after denying her return when Chico was on the way. But the old man was also the one who had made her paper boats on days of torrential rain, for them to launch down the little rivers that formed in the streets. It was he who came up with foolproof salves when she scraped her knees. And it was he, principally, who taught her about the heart, explaining the sound she heard in his chest when she leaned against his chest to sleep.

Father and daughter had always been mirror images of each other. He grunted, she grunted. He grew ornery, she grew ornery. He thought he knew everything, and she thought she knew everything, too.

This resemblance had been cause for Dona Ana's celebration. Each time another similarity appeared, she wrapped in a smile a *well done* that she never verbalized. Arguments with her husband were always the same: 'Why didn't you you stain the sheets on our honeymoon? Where was it you went wandering about when you were single? How can I be certain that Guida is my daughter?' Ana would respond timidly, saying that she'd never so much as hugged another man aside from her brothers, and in those early years she began to think that it was those hugs that had taken her virginity.

Later, when they established themselves in Rio, the greengrocer's prospered and they had some money for a private doctor, Ana sought out a specialist. She regretted having made the appointment as soon as the assistant called her name in the waiting room. With great effort, much hand-wringing, and a story that involved many facts but left out many exchanged words, Ana described her wedding night with enough clues for the doctor to reconstitute the scene.

The doctor was an immutable man, with glasses that made his eyes appear smaller and lips that never formed a smile. He was deeply interested in the fountain pen in his hands. He peered at the Parker as he responded to his patient, in the same dialect used by Ana. He told her that what had happened to her was quite possible, that not all women were born the same. That the private parts of some women were different from those of others, that an abundance of what's expected was not always in fact abundant – it could be minute, or nearly non-existent. That there was no reason to worry, for there was certainly something there that was imperceptible but real. That she would be all right and shouldn't think about that subject anymore, and that if she felt it was necessary he could recommend an elixir to help with her nerves.

When she returned to the store, Manuel asked how the doctor's visit had gone.

'He said that these ailments are a matter of age and that there's no reason for us to worry.'

She told her husband about the purchase of the elixir as she tied her apron over her clothes and walked to the other corner of the store. Explaining to her husband the true motive for her visit to the doctor and his vague response was beyond what Ana could handle, and beyond what Manuel could handle hearing.

It was the passing of time that brought Ana's revenge. Guida looked as though she'd been born only of her father. The two had the same high cheekbones and the same pointy nose. They both needed to shake their feet to sleep and snored softly when they caught a cold. They needed to have another daughter for Ana to see herself in, and yes, she saw herself in Euridice. Especially when the girl cast a sad glance towards the window, as though thinking of all the experiences left to have and which would never be hers. Ana knew this feeling. It was squashed by this life spent in clogs, her world transformed into the opening and closing of the doors of the greengrocer's. She was as intelligent as Euridice but could never see beyond the dozens of tomatoes.

After Manuel rebuffed his daughter he felt a deep regret, that Portuguese sort of regret that involves not letting anyone ever discover what you're thinking. When Dona Ana died this feeling grew even stronger, and he became even more Portuguese, never letting anyone know about anything. Everything would be all right, as long as he could spend his days in the store, sitting in his usual spot behind the counter.

It was Guida who suggested she take care of her father when she learned of his stroke. She had been far away from Dona Ana when she died and had no desire to add to her guilt. 'We'll sort out our differences,' she promised Euridice.

Moving to Santa Teresa would be good for Guida, Antonio, and Chico. That year, sales at the store had fallen. Antonio attributed this to the opening of a bigger stationery store in the neighborhood, and Guida attributed it to the incident between Zélia and Antonio. The business was put up for sale, the money invested in some land, and the three of them installed themselves in the apartment above the greengrocer's, together with Senhor Manuel.

As the months passed, Senhor Manuel began to recover from his stroke, eventually reaching the point where no one knew whether he grunted because of the stroke or his grumpiness. The one who found the old man's attitude a lot of fun was Chico, who'd always wanted a grandfather. He liked to read the poems of Guerra Junqueiro – his favorites – to Manuel.

> *It is so sad to watch them fall,*
> *To see them scattered through the air,*
> *The illusions we once erected*
> *Over our mother's breasts, that eternal altar.*
>
> *We no longer even know how, nor when*
> *Our souls will one day come to rest!*
> *For our souls wander aimlessly and float amid*
> *The electric current of the seacrest.*

Chico pretended not to see his grandfather's moistening eyes. He went on thinking about that old man with the crooked lips, who had never done anything with his life but sell fruit and who liked, in his free time, to ponder the souls lost amid the sea's electric currents.

Euridice would come to visit them two or three times per week, with a sea-green turban on her head and the smell of mint on her lips. She couldn't come more often because she had begun her history degree at the Catholic University of Rio de Janeiro. She was an outstanding student during that first year, more-or-less outstanding in the second, an interested student in the third, and a cynic during the fourth. She continued to write a lot, and she took Chico to some of the student protests that occurred after the military coup of 1964.

The family came together on Sundays for lunch at Euridice's house. Senhor Manuel would sit on the sofa near the window and stare at the Atlantic for hours, perhaps in search of souls lost amid electric currents, perhaps thinking about Ana, perhaps looking at some young girl's rear – how could she wear such a short skirt? Things aren't the way they used to be. Cecilia more or less participated in these gatherings, listening less to the conversations and paying more attention to the ringing of the telephone. It could be a friend inviting her to the movies or – after one of those parties she was always going to – she thought it could be him, oh my God, it could be him! Afonso continued keeping most of his words to himself. He ate in silence and had a habit of breaking up with his girlfriends after taking them out in the car for one last encounter, parked in the deserted streets of São Conrado. Antonio was always in a good mood, whether looking at Guida or at Euridice. Chico read, ate, traded a few words with Euridice, and then left the table. Antenor became even more Antenorish. Full of himself, sure of everything, incapable of fault, and woe betide anyone who said that he had failed in any way – if everyone failed the way he did, Brazil would be a world power.

When the family moved to Ipanema, Maria continued working in the house, but she had to leave her job in the second year. It was her legs that hurt, she told them. Through some acquaintances, Euridice arranged for a doctor's consultation at the hospital. It seemed Maria would have to undergo an operation, but no one knew anything else. Antenor and Euridice couldn't keep a maid who couldn't clean above the refrigerator. They paid her severance, gave her a few more *cruzeiro* notes, and Maria disappeared into the world, as quietly as ever.

After the 1964 coup, Euridice began to write with greater agitation, evidenced by the increased intensity of the *tack-tack-tack* of the typewriter. She sent a few texts to the *Jornal do Brasil*, which the newspaper never published. She tried out other newspapers, but never received a response.

Life in Ipanema, she soon discovered, wasn't so different from life in Tijuca. Sure, the sea brought in a refreshing breeze, and artists, journalists and writers could always be found discussing their ideas in bars, but still the unpleasant winds of rumors swept in as certain neighbors made their way down the sidewalk.

With a daughter who grew more different from her with each passing day, a son that was hers only because he had come out from between her legs, and a husband who came close only to kiss her on the forehead, Euridice retreated even further into herself, and into her book-lined study. She never took off her medallion of Our Lady, even after she stopped believing in God.

Life continued much in this way, and no matter what, a single sound could always be heard:

Tack-tack-tack, tack-tack-tack, tack-tack-tack…

Tack-tack-tack, tack-tack-tack, tack-tack-tack…

Tack-tack-tack, tack-tack-tack, tack-tack-tack…

AUTHOR'S NOTE

Who knows if one day Euridice's writing might receive its due. Perhaps, after the author's death, as Cecilia is tidying up Euridice's study alone (because Antenor is crying an ocean of tears that have been building since the day he saw Maria Rita's dead body), she will have time to leaf through the bound sheets of white paper locked away in the drawers.

Or perhaps it will be Chico, to whom Afonso and Cecilia will assign the task of organizing the study and keeping any books that catch his eye, on account of his closeness to his aunt.

Or perhaps it will even be Afonso, still beset by his mother's death, who, faced with organizing Euridice's closet or her papers, will say, 'I want to take care of her papers, Cecilia can have the closet!' in the vain illusion that this will allow him to keep a greater distance from his mother's scent.

Or Guida, summoned by Afonso and Cecilia to see after Euridice's things, since if it were possible they would appeal to their own mother for help in such a painful activity and instead run to their aunt in their mother's absence.

(But it couldn't be Antenor. He won't be able to cast an eye towards anything that belonged to Euridice, lest his eyes begin to stream again as he mutters, 'Euridice was a great woman,' over and over.)

At any rate, if someone, someday, peeks into the large desk drawer to find the bound white leafs of paper with a first page that reads *The History of Invisibility*, and if this someone has the patience and the wisdom to read those pages, they will quickly understand that Euridice's book is too important to belong to a single library alone.

ACKNOWLEDGMENTS

I am deeply grateful to my agent Luciana Villas-Boas, and to Anna Luiza Cardoso and Lara Berruezo, for their sustained support and profound love for Brazilian literature.

My translator Eric Becker should be mentioned for the same reason – one should be deeply in love with a language and a country to be able to translate its stories to the world.

I would also like to thank Marleen Seegers, from 2 Seas Literary Agency, for finding the perfect home for my book. I feel extremely lucky to work with the outstanding team at Oneworld. Thank you, Juliet Mabey, for bringing me to your very special publishing house. Thank you, Alyson Coombes, for all your support during the different stages of the translation and editorial work. And thank you to everyone else at Oneworld who has helped make this journey possible.

The copy-editor Will Atkins and publicists Becky Kraemer and Kate Bland should also be mentioned, for their professionalism and care towards this book.

Finally, I want to thank my husband Juan, for grounding my life and work as a writer.

MORE WORLD FICTION FROM ONEWORLD

The Unit by Ninni Holmqvist (Swedish)
Translated by Marlaine Delargy

Twice Born by Margaret Mazzantini (Italian)
Translated by Ann Gagliardi

Things We Left Unsaid by Zoya Pirzad (Persian)
Translated by Franklin Lewis

Revolution Street by Amir Cheheltan (Arabic)
Translated by Paul Sprachman

The Space Between Us by Zoya Pirzad (Persian)
Translated by Amy Motlagh

The Hen Who Dreamed She Could Fly by Sun-mi Hwang
(Korean) Translated by Chi-Young Kim

The Hilltop by Assaf Gavron (Hebrew)
Translated by Steven Cohen

Morning Sea by Margaret Mazzantini (Italian)
Translated by Ann Gagliardi

A Perfect Crime by A Yi (Chinese)
Translated by Anna Holmwood

The Meursault Investigation by Kamel Daoud (French)
Translated by John Cullen

Minus Me by Ingelin Røssland (YA) (Norwegian)
Translated by Deborah Dawkin

Laurus by Eugene Vodolazkin (Russian)
Translated by Lisa C. Hayden

Masha Regina by Vadim Levental (Russian)
Translated by Lisa C. Hayden

French Concession by Xiao Bai (Chinese)
Translated by Chenxin Jiang

The Sky Over Lima by Juan Gómez Bárcena (Spanish)
Translated by Andrea Rosenberg

A Very Special Year by Thomas Montasser (German)
Translated by Jamie Bulloch

Umami by Laia Jufresa (Spanish)
Translated by Sophie Hughes

The Hermit by Thomas Rydahl (Danish)
Translated by K.E. Semmel

The Peculiar Life of a Lonely Postman by Denis Thériault
(French) Translated by Liedewy Hawke

Three Envelopes by Nir Hezroni (Hebrew)
Translated by Steven Cohen

Fever Dream by Samanta Schweblin (Spanish)
Translated by Megan McDowell

The Postman's Fiancée by Denis Thériault (French)
Translated by John Cullen

Frankenstein in Baghdad by Ahmed Saadawi (Arabic)
Translated by Jonathan Wright

The Invisible Life of Euridice Gusmao by Martha Batalha
(Brazilian Portuguese) Translated by Eric M. B. Becker

The Temptation to Be Happy by Lorenzo Marone
(Italian) Translated by Shaun Whiteside

Sweet Bean Paste by Durian Sukegawa (Japanese)
Translated by Alison Watts

They Know Not What They Do by Jussi Valtonen (Finnish)
Translated by Kristian London
